A dyed-in-the-wool bo
in six states in ten years
press operator, phone sex actress, and
received her MFA from the School of the Art Institute of Chicago. She lives with her ex-fiancé's ex-mistress and pet rat. A collection of her short stories will appear in 2001.

Homecoming

CAREN GUSSOFF

SERPENT'S TAIL

Permission to reprint lyrics from 'Cease to exist' and 'You'll think I'm dead' from the Pixies' album *Doolittle*, written by Black Francis and published by Rice and Beans Music, is gratefully acknowledged.

Library of Congress Catalog Card Number: 00-102178

A complete catalogue record for this book can be obtained from the British Library on request

First published in 2000 by Serpent's Tail
4 Blackstock Mews, London N4 2BT

website: www.serpentstail.com

Typeset by Avon Dataset Ltd, Bidford on Avon, B50 4JH

Printed in Great Britain by Mackays of Chatham plc, Kent

10 9 8 7 6 5 4 3 2 1

In memory of Susan Grace
1959–1994

EPILOGUE

Reese was twenty-six when she decided watching sports was a good thing.

She might have started earlier; she left home eight years ago, but she never watched them before and at no time mentioned them since, so as far as I know, this was a new development.

It was a Tuesday afternoon in October when they found her. A cold snap pressed over the city that day, the front windows open; when the cops collected her body their mouths blew out frost. Time of death was estimated at or around 2 pm, Sunday, October fifteenth.

They noted the TV was on, tuned to a major network. There was nothing but football. It would have been the last quarter of the game. I looked it up; Broncos up Green Bay, thirteen to zero.

There is a photograph of Reese holding me. She's five years old and holds me up and out, like a garbage bag about to break. I'm all baby black hair and creased as a brain.

There is only one other photograph of the two of us

together. Nine years old, I am dressed like a tiger on Hallowe'en, face is painted yellow and fly wide open. Reese is a shadow on the left.

Already, by this time, our older sister couldn't suffer being looked at straight on.

The album had been a wedding present to our parents. It is cheap leather, stamped in gold like a bible, now saffroned by fingertips. It sits on a shelf gathering a damp membrane of dust and neglect. I'm the only one now who opens it, each time I visit our parents, flipping its pages. I search through it always, the only change the yellow space where the two photos of Reese and me lay before I stole them.

There are pictures of me: accumulations of successive grade school photos, I pose in front of autumn leaves, trains speeding into mountain passes, a boat balanced on top of a Great Lake. My eyes are unfocused, as if I were watching television. I try to remember what I was thinking in each, if my smile was sincere, how I kept from blinking. There I am: untouchable, assembled as a diorama, printed on only one side.

But most of these photos are of our younger sister Shay: a toddler, soft ankles yielding dangerously outward, our father's hands, like crutches, slipped under her arms; a faraway dab onstage at a Forensics tournament; and two years ago, holding an ice cream cone aloft like a torch, in a toast, her acceptance letter to pharmacy school across her lap.

These shots of Shay are candid and spontaneous. Her

brows are deliberative, a smile tows at her mouth. In our family, only Reese and I were close. When I think of Shay, she stands like an exchange student at the margins of a clique: polite, retiring, weary of interpreting. She nods at the wrong times, her laughter off and outlasting ours. I think of her squirreled away with projects, penpals, fat nonfiction books.

But here, she's taller, larger. Only the camera sees her fierceness. So substantial, staring up from the album, barely contained in the film, that I have to believe it.

I have a recurring dream. I drive across the desert. The windows are rolled down all the way. Light forks through the sunroof like a religious painting. I have the two photos of us on the seat beside me and a single blast carries them out the window. I watch them out the rear view mirror; they float, shouldered by the wind, then settle on the dunes that brim the highway. They catch the sun, glittering, and send up mirages. I like to think of them there. They reflect, betray an oasis.

I am angry at Reese for leaving me alone, but really, in my way, I've always been alone.

Really, this begins years ago, before this; it begins before she dies. It begins with me.

ONE

Late October rain hangs in the air, not quite falling, covering the bus windows with a unhappy gloss. It is afternoon, a Wednesday: I ride the number twenty bus toward our hometown, watching through the windows the world changing suddenly. We follow the powerlines north to Route eight, leaving the proportions of the city bordered by our hometown: the tight fleabags uptown, the doorless cars, and salsa, the palatial brownstone bluffs by the park. Then Route eight changes to Central Avenue at the limits of town. Rows of close plank houses and tar roofs line the streets, built without basements by the WPA, small Italian box gardens of basil, tomatoes pendulant on balsa wood posts, St. Francis under a bathtub grotto, a swingset.

The scenery is blurred, as if my hometown were itself surfacing from beneath a black ocean, the streets like slides projected down a hallway bordered by those houses, tight as lockers. No one can see me watching.

Downtown behind me, the bus follows the river. Industry, like agriculture, relies on water, and my hometown hems its river, cheerless, polluted. The racetrack now looms off to the left; I smell it before it rolls into view, wool and loam, beer, shifting to butter, upwind of the cookie factory, vanilla, tranquil though the smoke suggests otherwise. In the teachers' parking lot of Theodore Roosevelt, not my old school, this one in a better area, one blackberry tree breaks through the asphalt. And the shopping center, the Sanitary Fish Market somehow staying in business. Then the Post Office, the plaster Doric columns, and I look, an involuntary reaction, to catch the flat roof of the two-story clapboard our parents still, after all this time, rent.

There's not been a reason for me to go home. I don't think of home, and if I did, I'd really be thinking of Reese, although any thinking of Reese involves her leaving. If I thought of home, I'd think of her leaving, then how every day I wondered where she was, what she was doing, until one day I stopped. And if I thought of home, home itself, decorated so only two people can be comfortably in one place, three if someone stands, there still would seem to be nothing, no reasons to visit. Our parents' house seems a place full of history—simple furnishings made complicated, shrouded with doilies and shawls, imitation Fabergé eggs, baskets of multi-sized glass balls, Christmas cards a decade old sagging on countertops, coupons and clippings piled dangerously high in corners, elaborate floor urns of dusty silk flowers patterning a pinball-like maze through the rooms—but it is expressionless as to make your ribs hurt.

When Reese left, there seemed not much room for me, not much for me, and so I simply waited, scratching word puzzles in the Sunday papers until college.

And nothing's really changed in the two years I've been gone, at least that I can tell. This town fertile with memorized places. All the places I've been since, I can flinch a millisecond before each pothole, prophesy every corner and stoplight.

This was the center of the world and I swore I'd never return, no hard feelings. I lean back in the seat and narrow my eyes, dirty wind on my face from the window, let the landscape smudge, come to myself.

This was a trick I learned recently: I'm on the back of a motorcycle driving through Boulder. I'm holding onto my boyfriend, a man I'm not sure loves me. He is cussing into the blast, I can feel this through his back. We turn the wrong way down Baseline; he's driving too fast, and the turns bank the road. The world becomes dim and indistinct, a house is the same as the Flatirons fencing us from Utah, the same as a park, and I give myself to those curves, I give myself.

What happened was: I fight with the man I'm not sure loves me right before I leave. He has a name, it doesn't matter. All this I try to tell him, we lie in bed, he presses his palm into my stomach, I'm naked and he is not. If he listens, I don't know. He doesn't make a sound, he watches me smoke a cigarette to its filter.

What was different about this man with the motorcycle was one thing. He tried to show me the desert and I followed. We moved by month to different places, desert places, cheap apartments, carriage houses, a motel attached to a steakhouse. The strong, dry sun spread our memories bald, the top of skin into ashes, our faces settling into different features. Things disappeared, everything distilled, burning off under this heat, quickly. Evaporation was the only thing he believed in, he said. It was important I understand. When we were courting, he filled a glass with tap water and placed it on the window sill.

He said, Give it an hour.

I don't remember where this was, Texas, Arizona, but he smiled at me and spread out a newspaper.

Here, he said. Pick a movie.

What happened was: I fight with the man before I leave. I'm peeling a potato when the phone rings. I throw it across the room, it hits the refrigerator and rolls across the linoleum. I sit on the couch with a magazine like I don't know to read it, like I'm expecting someone. I sit there until the sun moves across my lap. I'm surprised when he comes home from work, one of his jobs, maybe as a valet, or a waiter.

He picks up the potato with a paper towel and brings it to me. Already the desert sun opened it, it's glazed with life, knotty with buds.

What is this? he asks; it sounds like a demand.

A potato, I answer. I was going to make dinner.

He rolls his eyes. It's disgusting, he says, and tosses it in the trash. Is there anything else to eat?

Later that night, I am naked, he is not. I stare at the wallpaper, illuminated by light from the street. I wonder if I'll remember it, a gray-blue pattern, the way it moves in the darkness, and I study it, memorizing as if for an exam. I stare until I feel a nosebleed start, thick and warm on my lip, and I remember it is Tuesday. The garbage men would come in a few hours, bring the potato to the dump. Its warty stems would shrivel, mummify. I feel tender towards it. I sit up and stab out my cigarette in the dark.

Goodbye, I say. I'm leaving.

TWO

A single black hair lays across Squid's cheese danish. He holds it to his mouth and bites, not noticing, and when he does, I shudder.

"We're not so different, you and me," he says, settling back in the booth. He places the danish down, and we face each other. "Everyone else our age getting married, having babies, working for the man. I've gone into business for myself."

He stretches, arching his back, then scratches his chest and belly. I can see the butt outline of the Beretta tucked into his pants, and he catches me looking. "And you, Katey? What you doing now?"

"I'm not sticking up friends from high school," I say. "How much you make doing that?"

"Oh, come on. If I'd seen it was you, I'd have asked nicely." He draws in his lips and sucks. "Besides, it don't shoot. At least not that I know of."

I look at my plate. I feel nauseous.

"When you'd get in?" he asks.

"Just now," I say. "First thing that happens you poke me with a gun."

This pleases him. "Come on," he says. "That's now the past. What you been doing?"

"College," I answer. "Then Section Eight. Out west. Then I was in Vegas."

"Vegas?"

I nod.

"You win?" he asks.

"Sometimes. Not always."

"I'm making more than you then. From the back, you look like you'd got money."

I look down at myself: hooded sweatshirt, my favorite, a Champion, faded teal from navy; blue jeans, the man with the motorcycle's, worn down to suede; artless black boots. My army backpack under the table.

"Can't have my rock and roll lifestyle on four hundred bucks a month," he says.

"Four fifty eight," I say. "And food stamps. It's not so bad. You live."

"Not enough for this." He rolls up his sleeves and holds out his arms, as if to receive a bouquet of flowers. They're bruised. The hairs look bleached against the purple skin.

"That's the slow way to do it," I say, shrugging.

He smiles at me, slits open a sugar packet and pours a pile on the table. "Some nights, I can make, four, five grand." He looks proud. He is lying. "You just gotta know what you're doing. You just gotta be smart."

"You need a partner?"

"That's what I'm saying."

I lean in towards him. A sweet mildew rises from his skin. "Does your mother know what you're doing?"

He takes another bite of the danish and tilts his head. "Does yours?"

It's a joke, but neither of us laughs. He finishes chewing, then holds up his coffee cup. "So. Tell me, Katey, what you doing back?"

I open my mouth, then shut it and shrug again, but he isn't watching. He looks past my shoulders. In spite of everything, he's beautiful. Heroin's sunk his skin close to the skeleton, tight and smooth. Delicate, you could destroy him with a match. But I've seen this before. It doesn't last. Before long, he'll grow jumpy and twisted, but for now his eyes are the same blue, his hair as blonde, pruned in hunks across his forehead, still as handsome as the time we drank so much mescal at Lara's summer house when I sat on the porch swing hallucinating I had a third leg growing from my belly, knee up. I'd thought Lara was on the driveway breaking bottles because she found out he and I messed around but she didn't know or didn't care. She was breaking bottles because someone ate the worm and it was her turn. When the bottles were gone, she picked up gravel and threw it, then stood still and studied something in her palm. You all gotta see this, she called. This rock here looks like a goddam potato. I lifted my head weakly. The leg was still there, the foot wearing a different sneaker than me. I tried to point it out to them, but Lara rolled that rock back and forth and Squid carried me to the toilet and held me while I peed, wiping me gently, not noticing the foot booting him square in the ribs.

But it won't last; I've seen this before. Reese had this

same look, that last time. Her eyes as she tried to kill me. This same look, like an angel of some sort or another. Beautiful, desperate, and hungry. Endlessly hungry.

"My mother," he says. "I haven't told her anything. Two years now."

"Me neither." I shake my head and drop a bill next to the check. "I should go."

He nods. Shay's address is written in blue marker on my hand. "You know where this is?" I ask.

"Don't," he says, gallantly. "Don't tell me where you live."

*

A two-story cinderblock on a macadam street, a grove of charred couches, no trees, just the smell of the river and a view of the housing projects in the distance, spiring over the matchbox family homes. Shay said yellow, but the building is grimed with exhaust and mineral deposits from the rain and I have to hold up the corner of my shirt and wipe at it. I figure her window is a basement corner apartment at kneeling level and I knock on the glass even though the lights are out. The next-door window opens and a guy's head pokes out. He looks at me and I set my backpack down.

"She's not home," he says. "She's downtown. At class."

"She didn't know I was getting in." I lean against the wall. It wasn't like I expected a homecoming. "I don't think she's at class."

He holds up a finger, then slides aside the screen and climbs out. He's pale, wearing khaki shorts and a white baseball hat. "So," he says.

"I'm Shay's sister," I explain.

"Really." He looks me up and down. "When'd you get here?"

I look down at my wrist and remember I'm not wearing a watch. "This morning."

He leans up next to me. We watch the parking lot. Nothing stirs. "What did you do?" he asks. His voice is very quiet.

"Some dancing," I say. "Mostly dealing."

"Oh yeah?" He glances at me and grins. I notice a rosy blotch edging his cheeks. He's got me, he thinks. I can feel him think, Now I've got you. "What was it like?"

"Hot," I say. "I wish I were still there." This seems to be the truth, even though I can't exactly remember why.

He moves closer to me and holds out an arm. "It's not so bad out here."

"No," I answer. "It's not so bad."

He cups his other hand around my breast. His touch fills the air like humidity. I'm aware of nothing else. I try to remember if Shay ever wrote of any friends or steadies or anything. "Who are you?" I ask.

"Danny," he says. "Danny."

In Danny's bed, I hear her: Shay, TV noise, an answering machine above it, and she sings to herself. Her movements unseen but reverberating: a closet door, bag of groceries, a six pack of Cokes or juice boxes, and who can blame her, for what we've been through, and she doesn't know, she doesn't know anything.

And here I am: I listen, roll out from under Danny's arms, half under his chest, and listen. Our younger sister Shay moves heavily. She kicks off her shoes, settles on her futon, and the TV goes up, the Discovery channel special on Anastasia Romanov; I know because I've seen it already. I get up, open his fridge; there are pears. I take three of them, pour myself some coffee, the pot barely warm, and drink it from an ugly little mug that says *DANIEL: Lion of God* in carnival script. Sitting cross-legged on the floor, I listen. She's tired, there is no more movement, nothing but a commercial now.

Danny turns in his sleep and I look at myself in the weak light. I sparkle with his sweat and I can't face Shay now, not this minute, can't tell her the news about Reese. I suddenly want to get out of here. My heart beats, and I decide I'm going to go see Annika instead and I feel for my clothes, my shoes, and feel like I should kiss Danny goodbye and I almost don't. He always wanted to fuck a girl like me, he didn't have to say that out loud but I know. I didn't have the heart to tell him he was wrong, if he was wrong. What could I have said? Dancing and dealing, sure, but dance instructor and blackjack dealer to make ends meet, any job I could find moving town to town, but today, I could have called Shay from a pay phone, gone to a bookstore instead, or the market, sat outside and smoked an entire pack of cigarettes. Danny isn't awake, and I don't want him to be, but then I do, and under my lips his freckled eyelids feel like fruit that should have been refrigerated. He's too soft and doesn't move.

I look at his face, try to memorize it, commit the nose, parted lips, but when I look away, I can already remember him only in concepts, in colors.

I do not love Danny.

Before I climb out the window, I leave a dollar and a note. Thanks, I write, for the pears.

I've always been partial to boys with freckles. Their skin, the filaments of their muscles underneath, like fish, the peach and carmine undertones. Flushed, dappled Irish boys with mothers and Eagle Scout knives, Pintos, bony knees. Boys like orchids who blanch in the sun.

There is a boy like that on the bus to Annika's, another boy; he sits one row up, one row across. He doesn't notice me, but when he gets up for his stop, he smiles at me in an offhand way. I feel abandoned. I've been staring at him so long, I felt like we were together.

These are not the men I know.

The men I know have tongues dark as Labrador retrievers. The men I date have eyes darker than their pupils. They are wanting, small and dark and lash boys with austere tendencies. Boys who feel sorry, always deeply sorry, sincere in their asceticism, their wishes to become rock stars, labor union organizers, to only purchase rennetless cheese. My men have motorcycles, think they have something to show me. My men and I wait like poachers, moving our camps after a ghostly herd; they point into the distance, stare out into the light and hope to see the dead move again.

I understand.

My men have no other place to put themselves except where the earth itself is as thirsty as they are.

It was easy for me to love the man with the motorcycle. I followed him. His hands were thin and pointed. He worried deeply about drought, and debt, and the overprescription of penicillin. He thought me precious as a responsibility.

This man, he told me I'm only hurting myself.

I can see him, underside my lids. The wrinkles, hairs, a glazed scar throat to chin. Sixty lower lashes, left eye, which is, I estimated, two millimeters smaller than the other. Pinhole nostrils bowed, a yin and yang.

And all this disquiet he felt, he felt enough for the two of us, a feeling he thought I should share.

You're only, he said, shaking his head, hurting yourself.

And so, I'm not sure if he loves me.

Love, I think, is in the details.

Yesterday, before I leave for the bus station, I buy and install an air conditioner. It has ruffled panels that accordion out to block the window. I tear up the receipt, and turn it up to high. I sit in front of it, watching the bearded filter shiver, and pack. I leave him a note too, this man I'm not sure loves me, and the A/C instruction book.

Shouldn't we have had one of these, I write, all this time.

★

Six years ago. This is the last time I see our sister Reese alive.

It is 90 degrees, August, the month draped off from the rest of the year by humidity; gorged doors opening only with a kick to the bottom left, paper swollen and plush as denim. It is the time of the year when even your body feels glut and clogged, stiff, not like a muscle man stiff, but as if you have too much blood in your veins. I am seventeen. I hold up my arm, Reese beats at me, palm side out.

You come here, you little shit, she screams, with seven dollars in your pocket? I know you got more.

She glows and sweats, holds my head out the window, the train tracks scattering sunlight across the street like seeds.

Should I break your neck? she asks, but then her boyfriend grabs her hair into a ponytail and pulls us back, calms her with a baggy of speed, white crosses, pulled from his pocket.

Jimmie. That one's name was Jimmie, and he saved my life. He was the last one before she went on the streets, or before I stopped paying attention. Jimmie, the kind of guy who lifted weights because he thought the world was laughing at him. He owned some kind of snake. A boa constrictor. Reese called and asked for money, begged me to come over, or he was going to have to sell the boa constrictor. There was panic in her voice. Please, she said. I remember she said once that when Jimmie was angry, he'd beat her with it, threaten to starve it then hook it around her neck, around her waist, right above the liver. When he wasn't angry, he'd leave it in the bed while they had sex, when they had sex, stretched out like an arm, adhering to the sweat on her back, in heaven with the heat, the damp.

The second to last visit, Jimmie sits on a bag of soda cans to return for deposit, I sit on a lawnchair in the middle of the room. He offers me a drink. The snake wrapped around his leg like a tourniquet. His hand over my hand, brushing my wrist, catching hold, wrapping my fingers around a can of orange soda.

Unless, he says, leering, you'd like something hard.

I rub at the damp rings from the can into the thighs of my jeans. I feel him watching me watch my sister sleep.

It was nice of you to come see us, he says.

To me it is obvious that I hate him, that there is no us beyond Reese and me, but I don't answer and I don't look at him. We sit uncomfortably in silence for awhile. He coughs and I give in. I feel sorry for him, after all, his ridiculous black dress shoes, the rings under his eyes. I finally look over at him, and he runs his tongue over his teeth.

You as much of a hellcat as your sister? he asks.

I stare at Reese, willing her to wake up. When we were children, a cough would send her into my room, over to my bed, slapping for me in the dark, hissing, I'm trying to sleep, dammit, Katherine. No one ever calls me

Katherine, no one ever did, except Reese and only in the night. Reese never slept that I remembered, not much. Sometimes, I think it was the speed—Reese vacuuming the downstairs, dying her hair, she even learned to can vegetables—and then I think sometimes, it was something else. Morning light climbing upwards, she'd slip into bed with me, smelling like smoke, entwining our legs, my pajama bottoms catching on her stubble. When I'd awaken, she'd be gone, and I could never tell if she'd actually been there at all. She left no marks, no evidence: a hair, a scratch, a smell—all of which could have been mine, been an accident. My older sister if she slept, never dreamt, this is what she told me. But this day she slept, blissful, loose, her lips moving to a song I couldn't hear. Jimmie wiping at his face with his T-shirt hem, he kicks at her shin lightly. She rolls across the mattress, her eyelids open like incisions showing white bone, and snores softly. He looks over at me.

Don't look at me like you don't know what I'm talking about. He claws the air. Are you a hellcat like your sister?

No, I mumble. No, I'm not.

That last time, he pokes his tongue in Reese's ear, saying, There you go, baby. We're all right.

He mashes five or six pills with a dirty fork into powder, and watches as she snorts it straight off the table top. He doesn't offer me any. I realize it's not what I thought, it's Pervitin, Pivo, the inhale of the Kamikazes courtesy of the Nazis. Cheaper than crack, than crystal, it is imported from Baltic labs, they're really in trouble, really don't have any money. Reese wipes at her nose, sweatshirt sleeves dangling past her fists, too taut, punchy, the mimic of a sleepy gesture. I watch her face tensely, she looks composed, but I wait for her expression to change. We're sweating, the heat and the room makes us seem as though we are standing closer together than we are, a gluey moment, lasting forever. This is how I will remember her face. She chews at the inside of her cheeks and studies me, I meet her eyes, reach out to touch her. She clamps her hands over her ears and howls, pants, pulls back, a rodent, a scared rodent. Her eyes are filled, her mouth is open, she's about to say something.

She says, Katey, out of the corner of her mouth. She says she was counting on me.

She says, Give me your earrings, my small ruby studs, not even 14 karat, just 10, Give them to me.

She says, I diapered you, you give them to me, the pitch growing, hysterical, she has to get my earrings, her face has changed. She knocks me, I fall, crashing into something, my head is between her legs, she holds my head, she rips my earlobes. She says, Get out. I lean against the wall and shut my eyes. The smell of chickens frying and nothing more.

*

If you ask our mother, everything was lost in the fire.

That was when everything changed. It happened when she was pregnant with me. All her grandmother's recipes, my father's army passport with a stamp from Ceylon, a knotted wood shillelagh, letters, all of Reese's toys.

And the replacements are never right, she said frequently, frowning at a roast. My family watched the fire from the street, the house curling at the edges like it was made of paper. I was born six months later.

Did you feel anything? Can you remember that? Reese asked me once, The fire, the heat? And I don't. I don't remember anything, but I can see them like that, just the three. Reese placed her hands on my mother's belly, our father held the photo album above his head, smoke poured backwards from a hole in the sky.

Nothing's been right since, my mother says, poking the meat as if it were at fault.

It's too tough to chew, she says.

Maybe things were different before. There is no way I could remember. Ash fell like rain, they brushed it from their hair.

Our parents never wore wedding rings. I asked about it once, when I was old enough to notice but too young to figure what it meant. My mother said they were lost in that fire, and when I opened my mouth to ask why they weren't on their fingers then, my father shook his head, wordlessly. It's no use, he seemed to be saying. That's the way it is. My mother slapped my hand from my mouth.

Stop chewing your cuticles, she said. We know we're

married. We don't need rings to keep us together. We've got all of you.

★

I can't imagine the moment of Reese's death. Of all the bad things I've done, I am only half as bad as her, and maybe I have tried. I've held a gun; the first time, my friend Michael and I shot his .357 at a live oak outside the tattoo storefront in the middle of the night. It was finals week, and at the university, in the town, it was tradition. Midnight displayed hundreds of thousands of us screaming, yelling, and crying. I met him at the shop and we fired, my hands under his, and it knocked me back against his chest, dumb at its weight. The bough, broad as a thigh, grew soft and flushed with water rot. Soon after, it withered and I left with the man and the motorcycle before the city removed the tree.

Reese taught me everything, and I believed her. I knew nothing else.

Not to eat restaurant coleslaw, how to comb out hickeys, how to make a slug. To smear white liner to make your eyes look larger. That if a boy can't keep his hands off you, to pick your nose, and if he still won't, to eat it. If he sticks you in the trunk of his car, to cut the tail-light wires and hope for the best. Vodka and lemon juice give long lasting highlights.

These are the things she'd tell me in the night.

If you know you're going to be frisked at the door,

hide a razor under your tongue. The best way to shoplift is to empty your purse to look for something. Grab the item, shove it back in with your wallet, your keys. Write the answers to a final exam, pressing hard, on a stack of loose-leaf paper. They'll engrave through the first few blank sheets.

I belonged to her. My first memories are of her, always of her, pressing her thumbnail into an X over a mosquito bite, pulling down my knee socks, playing the blue dot game on the vacuum tube TV. Reese and I switched the set off, the picture collapsing onto itself like a small moon, then on our haunches we'd chicken to see who'd wait the last second to flip it back on before the dot disappeared and the set had to warm up again. We played games no one could win.

And then once, when I am fourteen years old: Reese holds a fork to my cheek, matching the tines to my moles and jamming. She wanted to make me afraid, but I stared back, the prongs slipping, oily with icing. Our mother always said, Ugliness changes you inside, look away, when we'd pass a car accident or something on fire, she'd grip the steering wheel. Our mother couldn't stand pain, almost crashing the car, looking away. Shay'd shut her eyes tightly, but Reese'd watch and I'd watch Reese watching. Reese was a watcher, and sometimes I understood what our mother meant. Watching is a sort of participation. My sister Reese grew to hate touch, to be looked at at all, but always she watched. She lived with the shades pulled, darting out under people's stares. This day with the fork I wasn't afraid.

I didn't flinch, I looked right at her, daring her.

Stab me, I said. Do it.

This was what she was training me for.

She drew away, put the fork down, saying, I'm the big sister, tore at the lemon cake with her fingers. Reese always ate sweet stuff, and I learned later all junkies did, devouring what they could stomach between fixes, their eyes burnished and edgy. I saw them all the time in diners. They'd enter in groups and sit apart, backs taut with urgency as they ordered milkshakes, bear claws, and soggy pies. They'd gulp cokes, alarmed at the feel of their own arms, tactile, brushing at their sides.

Reese taught me everything and I listened; I was Reese's little girl until I helped her pack her things in garbage bags.

But this isn't exactly true. We were all four years apart. Our mother had us evenly spaced out, even to the month, like seasonal fruits. She wanted us to take care of one another, not to compete. She herself was an only child and wished for a sister, every day, she said, and looked at us so lovingly that it seemed sheer will we were all girls, her girls. She looked at us so lovingly that I don't know what she saw.

Reese was not beautiful. She had the vague outlines of my family, the beefy curves, and eyebrows like a man. She was prone to bruising. This is not what I was thinking yesterday afternoon when the phone rang. First: I was thinking of a cheese grater, to shred some hash browns. I couldn't find it in the kitchen drawers, the utility closet, or the dishwasher. The officer had a Jamaican accent.

He tells me his name. He tells me to call him Bill.

We have a body, he says.

He says something about forensics. I think of children, a line of children, notecards, tiny Adam's apples quivering. Forensics, the art of speaking. I think of Shay's trophy. Then I'm not thinking of anything at all. I listen. He says, Shot. He says, Two in her sternum and one in her zygoma.

That means her face, doesn't it? I ask.

Bill seems surprised. Yes, he says. That's when I think she was the most beautiful woman in the world.

★

I have tried to remember the fire, or being born, or the first time I was deposited into Reese's arms. I don't know the old house, know the way things were, if this deposit was a loan or a gift.

I was given to Reese. Then our father lost his job, then another. He wasn't a self-starter, wasn't a drinker or a beater: our father stared into the television, then the walls.

But nothing could fail our mother's plans. Shay came, and the clapboard rental, all of us. We learned you can't own things, objects, collections. They disappear, get taken away, through heat, through fire, through time.

What you can't bring back. And all the things you think are permanent.

Our parents were children of the Depression. Other details of their youth are dim.

Our father remembered when wax paper was worth something. Our mother was raised in foster care. The woman she stayed with gave out matches on Hallowe'en.

This led to many fights between them, and silence between us all. Our father watched the walls like windows while our mother searched for perfection. Each new thing would untangle the stomach, mollify the heart. She believed this, surrounded herself with objects. There would be no more want.

How could we not afford this?

Then, objects would fail, be discarded, consumed, or collected; the house building up into a shrine, like *nicho* stuffed with saints, toys, and candles lining the sides of New Mexican roads commemorating terrible car accidents, urging us to remember.

And our mother would begin again, adding another layer, complaining, The replacements are never right, even though no one, by now, remembers the originals.

And as for us, the daughters: we also each had uses, assigned roles. This is not uncommon in families. Reese was the one to worry about, and Shay, accomplished. Our mother moving silently through the house, waiting for Reese, checking the phone receiver. Early mornings, our mother arranging crêpe and roses across Shay's door, balloons that read *Congratulations*.

There is another photograph in the album, one that

explains my place. I am four months old, five tops. I can only maybe crawl, and if that, not very well. However, I sit unsupported on an old orange loveseat. My smile is adult, tight, my posture erect, a still, tiny thing from Madame Tussaud's. This is how it was explained: our mother thought it a perfect shot, one to mail around, pass at bridge parties. Pillows would have gotten in the way. And so, our father affixed me there, duct-tape across my back.

Of all the things I've done, I've never kept our mother awake at night.

And our mother always wanted a sister. This she said, along with any other things. But always distracted, as if it were all happening right now, somewhere over my shoulders.

Our mother's obsessions were elsewhere. We were free to pursue our own.

★

Our parents hadn't talked to Reese in over a year. But our parents hadn't spoken to one another either, not as long as I could remember. This is not how we were.

We all talked, but of what, it was no consequence. Our mother didn't believe in pain, and blurred her eyes to it. If you cannot see, cannot hear, if it is not said, it doesn't exist. This is how you live a life.

How many times I let it go, when I'd mention Reese, how many times I granted our parents a change of subject. If I had a dollar for each time, a dime, things could be different. No welfare lines, no dealing, dancing, nothing. The motorcycle could be fixed, all sober plastic curves. I could have made it, wherever I was going.

A few months ago, I sent Reese a one-way ticket. She said she was on the street, I had to help her.

Please, she said, but she never came.

I bought the ticket cash, then waited at the Las Vegas station, drinking the free instant coffee. Buses announced, disembarked.

I could have sent her an airline ticket instead, all those dimes, all those instances, our father cracking the newspaper, mother applying more lipstick, Shay's and my voice nothing more than a feeble trickle, Don't we have to try again?

Our mother answers me, My blood sugar. You're raising my blood sugar, Katey.

She lets a seizure, crumpling backward a bit, biting for air until our father delivers a drink, a pill. Our mother takes to bed. I stand under everyone's eyes.

Never mind, I say to no one in particular. I'm sorry, but for what, I am not sure. Never mind, and then I am quiet. Silence is the worst lie.

Nights at our parents' house prowling the hallways, my hands wrapped around an empty cup. By my sides, they no longer feel natural.

I can't help thinking I could have saved her. I thought I could.

She had the train ticket on her body. My phone number, directions.

We'd found a number on her, Bill says. I'm calling it now.

Who are you? he asks.

⋆

When I search the photo album, I know what I am looking for. The ones never taken.

Her head bowed, hair tracing along her ears, roan with peroxide, Reese in a fringe jacket and tight black jeans on our parents' couch. It was the last Christmas she came. I was happy.

She could be so kind. Shay opens the little white box, a small band with two folded hands. It's called a fede ring, Reese says, It means friendship. It's Irish, and she smiles. Shay kisses her cheek. Then my box, a oval cameo, the profile ivory over rose shell, and she points at her chest and what's pinned there. Like me, she says, and I stroke it, then hug her, and she repeats, Just like me.

There was no camera. Reese'd be beaten for the gifts, lifted from a fence. She'd sneak into the house, stealing them back while we slept, but for that moment, we are happy, and I follow her into the bathroom.

I want to do my eyes like that, I say, and Reese laughs.

In a second, OK, just wait, she says, sitting on the edge of the bathtub.

She reaches inside her breastpocket and unfolds a square of tinfoil and a pipe she called her boiler, empties a square of salty powder onto the foil. She fumbles around.

You got a lighter? she asks, and I shake my head.

I know what she is doing. I expect her to be shy.

You're not a little kid anymore, she says.

And even though I wish I were, I shake my head. No, I say. I'm not.

Go get me matches, she says, quickly, the kitchen kind, the long ones, and I do, and sit on the toilet. She strikes the match on the lip of her boot and holds the flame under the foil, sucking up through the boiler. I wait to see if she offers me any; I wait to see what my answer will be. But this does not happen. Her eyes close and open, and I wait. She runs the pipe under cold water and balls the foil up. It takes less than a minute, and then she wets a fingertip under the faucet, faces me. From her back pocket she pulls a small vial of kohl, unscrews the top, rubs her finger across the surface.

To do your eyes, she says, hoarsely, sweep both lids together. The fringe tickles my cheeks, and I feel her fingers, familiar, this time not a dream.

There, she says, I'm finished.

When I open my eyes, I am beautiful.

★

I became a different type of addict. Desperate to recall Monets, to hold them forever. I think of photos never taken, stills inside my head, and realize that nothing, no object in the world could hold these moments, that when I stare at my photographs this is what is missing. All I see is my own face, patterned back in raised dots, that I rub my fingers over.

I used to look just like Reese, and Shay, like me. We were seasonal fruits.

Every day for years Reese got me ready for the day, pulled my hair down with conditioner and braided it.

We have doll hair, thick and hollow, she'd say down to me, sitting between her knees, a ritual.

Both of us, she'd say. You and me. Dry like plastic.

She'd tug my forehead so I had to work to blink, then spin me around, and drive me to school. I felt like a doll, a mannequin. Shay had a boy cut, sleek and pulled to the side, easier on our mother's arthritis, and a short walk to the elementary school. I was relieved when Reese finally wrapped our mother's car around a tree. The number twenty bus left no time for braids, and I cut it short as Shay's. I was relieved my bangs caught fire off my third cigarette ever and didn't melt like plastic. I'm real, I thought to myself. I'm real.

She was beautiful to me, even before I hung up the phone with Bill, the homicide investigator. I'd never known anyone like Reese, maybe anyone but Reese.

I can't imagine the moment of her death, although I let

myself try. In the bathtub, I run my fingers over my ribs and try to imagine the snap of a bullet, then another, and another, warm water curding into my blood. I once read a headline about an old woman who froze to her linoleum as she knelt to pray. It was days before anyone found her there, sobbing Dear lord, dear lord, and it was days before anyone found Reese, before they identified her.

I almost asked Bill why they didn't send an officer, someone to my door, but who would want to tell me such news? Everyone has a daughter. I hear it all the time.

I have a daughter your age, they say tenderly, shopkeepers, bank tellers, bus drivers, until I move and they get a flash of tattoo or notice the rings in my ears. Then their faces grow hard, like I've betrayed them. But not like me, I think. I am alone.

I'll come, I said into the phone to Bill. I'm coming.

I run my fingers over my ribs and think of a photo of our mother that does exist in the album; strong and beautiful in a picture hat. I come back to that often. I like to think of myself there, somewhere under her thin sailor's dress, some time in the past, inculpable, a pearl white buoy, unrealized and possible, bobbing in sauce.

Of all the bad things I've done, not telling my family is the worst.

THREE

The bus drops me three blocks from Annika's. I hold the envelope from a Christmas card in my hand and check the address. She hears my boots on the porch.

"The door doesn't close," Annika calls. "The toilet doesn't work, except for number one."

I walk in and she blows on me immediately, cursing and saying "Jesus Christ, Jesus Christ."

I let her hug me tightly. "Katey. It's Katey," she murmurs, punching me lightly on the back.

"Number one," I mutter. "Christ. I'm not one of your third graders."

She unclasps her arms and stands back. "I can't hear you. You're muffled." She places her hand on her hip and grins. "What the fuck are you doing here?"

"Hello, Annika," I say.

She has a black eye. She points to it. "Beat down. Before you ask. I had to get a sub."

I wait for her to ask me how I am. She doesn't. I watch her toss laundry off the couch into the corner and sits down. "Did you win?" I ask her.

She laughs and pats the seat next to her. "At Flat Duo

Jets. Last night."

"You live for that rockabilly shit."

"Ha. Josh does." She looks at me thoughtfully and shakes a cigarette from a pack on the coffee table and lights it. "Your hair's grown." She inhales carefully and flicks into a can. "You look good." She balances the cigarette between her lips and smoothes down her bangs. I always wanted to wear my hair like Annika's. You need a strong face, strong features. That was Annika: arresting, irregular, her movements of someone who could have been a dancer but chose not to be, like someone who can still meet men as an elementary school teacher, the officially established least sexy profession. But she was back with Josh, who didn't have strong features, his nose in a permanent pucker to keep his glasses up, an array of differently colored Converse and an exhaustive, insatiable knowledge of useless things: female mass murderers, schwa theory, and Indie pop bands filled with boys like him—their complete discographies, and obscure record labels in Olympia, Vancouver, Portland, rainy places.

"You look better," I say. "You always do." I take a cigarette from her pack. "Except the eye. Can I have one of these?"

Annika waves her hand. "They patted me down, but you can put some hell damage with a mikestand."

"Any clubs left you're allowed in?"

She ignores me. "So this girl says, 'You're blowing smoke in my face,' and I go, 'So, that's your face?' Then some guy pushes back and she falls and grabs my tits."

"Yeah, only I can grab your tits."

"So there's this mikestand, what?"

"I said, Josh. Josh can. I don't know. I'm tired." I look around. Recycling or garbage in every corner, papers, ashtrays, IKEA entertainment centers, a dead marigold in a Guinness bottle. I walk up and study a framed poster. It's black and white: two sides of the same face posed to kiss. "That's new."

"Josh met Joel-Peter Witkin. He puked the whole time."

"Joel-Peter Witkin?"

"Josh." She sighed. "You know how he feels about Joel-Peter Witkin. And Arbus. Diane Arbus."

"The freak lady?"

Annika nods. I look at my face reflected in the glass.

"He's disgusting."

"Joel-Peter Witkin?"

I collapse back on the couch. "No. Josh."

Annika gives me the finger.

"Annika, you're number one too," I say.

She leans her head on my shoulder, then wrinkles her nose. "You smell like fucking."

"Nice to see you too."

"Seriously. What you been at?"

"I ate some cantaloupe today. By Shay's. And some pears."

"And before that?"

I shrug.

She lights another cigarette. "So what you got to do downtown?"

"Just errands."

"Fuck errands."

I get up and wander into the kitchen. "Have anything good? I'm starving." I open her cabinets. They're empty, free of dishes, glasses, anything. I open the fridge instead and just stand there.

"You hungry?" she asks.

"Annie, give me ten bucks, and I'll pay you tonight."

"What are you looking for?"

"I need it for errands. I know you got it. Please?"

"Ten bucks? You have no money?"

"No. I just got here."

"How did you get here?"

"Bus."

"How are you living?" she asks.

"Hey, at least I don't have to shit in a garbage bag and toss it down the disposal or whatever you've got to do. Eat off paper towels."

"Where you think my money comes from?"

"Your parents."

She looks furious. "Fuck you."

Annika's parents were wealthy alcoholics. She was ashamed. It wasn't until I left that I realized they weren't as wealthy as I thought, just better off than my parents, than most everyone else's parents I knew. We never talked about this. Her mother was head of the local Republican party, her father didn't seem to do anything except hit on me whenever he opened the door, which wasn't often. Most of the time Annika waited for me or all of us sitting on the porch swing, even in the snow. We'd drive up the river to the private girls' college which had recently gone coed, and shoot pool and pretend we went there which didn't fool any one of the four hundred students who actually did. We'd sit in the pub in our jean jackets and order veggie burgers, the main ingredient of which seemed to be beets. They'd dye our mouths and tongues a cheerful magenta that took days to wear off, except Tommy Marvette, who just drank coffee because his mother thought the dye was from some drug and wouldn't leave him alone. Mrs. Marvette would sniff all Marvette's clothes, even his boxers, which was good for a laugh. I asked him once if that counted as scoring. He'd wake up and she'd be pulling out a hair, threatening to send it to a lab.

My friends: we talked, but of what was no consequence.

This is how we were: moving together like pack animals, like the damned.

Annika goes back into the other room and sits down again. I go after her. She holds up a ten.

"I'll get it back to you, " I say. I take the money. "I'm good for it. I could always steal taps. Prowl around frat houses at night. Return them to the liquor store for the deposit."

"Steal taps." She laughs. "Just like old times."

"Old times?"

She laughs again and tucks her feet under her. I look at her.

Seventeen, eighteen years old, after some party, she and I were sitting up on a bridge. She told me about her foot. I'd never seen it, but she always said she slammed it in a door. The one night she spent in Juvie for playing mailbox baseball, some girl sliced off her littlest nail with a burnt plastic comb because she was rich and she was ashamed.

Where were the guards? I asked.

Annika tossed her bottle over the side. They held me down.

FOUR

Few facts are known of the last day of Reese's life. They say she was living with a hooker by then, maybe living as a hooker. A group of them lost a night of work waiting around the station for her, drinking free instant coffee. They were thinking maybe she'd been arrested. They waited for her most of the night, first two or three of them, then just one, named Kim, who slept on the molded seats. They say Kim had AIDS, looked like a Styrofoam packing peanut. Kim cried all night long.

They don't say this to me, the dispatcher with the pink glasses, the sergeant at the desk. It's as if I'm at the zoo. A restraining bar edges the section like a cage, the lead gray linoleum floor slopes downward to the desk like a moat around deadly animals. I white-knuckle the bar, going through ballet positions, point my toes horizontal, second position, splay my legs, and watch as if no one can see me, listen to what the officers say to one another loud enough for me to hear. I hold on and tuck my hips under. Third position, one foot behind the other, waiting for Detective William Keene, fourth position, step forward, fifth, fifth, I can't remember how that one goes and suddenly stand still.

Call me Bill, he said on the phone, and I want to laugh because he sounded so tender. I will always remember how he sounded.

These are not the men I know.

There's a buzz and a side door opens out to where I'm standing. Bill stands there, hat in his hand, with yellow hair and yellow eyes like a strange cat, a lynx. "Miss Bruscke?" he asks, pointing at me.

I nod, he waves for me to come in. I walk into the corridor. Behind me, the steel door slides and clicks.

Bill holds out his hand and I look at it. "I'm Detective Bill Keene," he says, and I take his hand, we shake, his hand is dry and tight with no hair on it anywhere and I blurt out "I thought you were Jamaican."

"No," he says. "South African." His eyebrows are woolly and paler than his face. "Will you follow me?"

I trail him into a small office. It's filled with furniture common to dentist offices, showroom facilities, and hotel suites: two padded chairs surfaced with woven fabric, a coffee table molded in one piece, a free-standing lamp. On the wall hangs an oil of two pale blue boats upon a ceremoniously darker lake, the sun an impossible orange daub. He sits down. I follow suit and he drags his chair knee to knee with mine.

We look at one another and he smiles, pulling a notebook from his pocket. His teeth are all the same length and very close together. "I'm just going to ask you a few questions," he says. "Name?"

"Katherine Bruscke."

He writes it down in cautious letters. "Bruscke?" he asks. "German?"

I try to think of wars or alliances between Germany and South Africa. "We're not sure."

He strokes his colorless brows. "Age?"

"My age? Twenty-two," I say. I wait for him to write that down, but he doesn't.

He places the notebook down between us. "Miss Bruscke," he says. "I am a homicide detective. Your number was found on the victim. So, we have some reason to believe you can . . ." he trails off, coughs, then continues, "help us out." He looks at me, first my eyes, then a spot somewhere on my forehead.

I cross my arms across my chest. "Am I a suspect?" I ask.

"No," he says. "You were in . . ." He looks at his notes. "Las Vegas, Nevada when the crime was committed." He meets my eyes again, pauses for a moment, then says, "But you were close to the victim."

"Reese," I say. "I'm her family."

"We have reason to believe this crime was a passion crime. Drug related. We are not placing in question any family members." He puts the notebook in his lap, and writes something down. "Did you know much about Reese's activities?" He places the pen in the spiral and leans forward. "Was she a passionate woman?"

A knock on the door, and a receptionist lets herself in. She carries a portfolio under one arm and a coffee set on a tray, setting both on the table. Bill places the folder on his lap, tipping a mug at me. "How do you take it?" he asks.

Bill opens the folder across his lap. "Reese Bruscke." He studies it, browses its contents. "Kim," he finally says. "Heard of Kim?"

I shake my head. "She was living with some Jimmie. Last time I saw her." I clear my throat. "Before it got bad."

"And then?"

"Then I don't know."

He drains his coffee cup. "Then you moved?"

"Out west."

"Nevada?"

"Colorado, New Mexico, Arizona. Nevada."

He holds up the pot of coffee to offer me a refill. "Why?"

"College," I answer.

He looks surprised. "So, you're a good kid."

I think about that. "No. I'm another one."

"These two photographs, they're the best you have?" Bill holds them out, then close to his face. His lower lip sags in concentration. "Well," he concludes, "you were precious."

"Frankly," Bill sighs, "she was lucky to live this long."

"I sent her a ticket," I explain, weakly. "I was going to save her."

*

Bill tells me he'll accompany me to the morgue.

He leads me to a patrol car, a real one, unlocks the door and holds it for me. I can't believe this is the first time I've ever been in a police car, that it looks like the inside of any American-made car, with a partition like a taxi. He slides into the driver's seat, and it seems to start without a key, and I stare at him but he looks straight ahead.

He says this isn't the way they like to do things, and I nod. He says if we can do a positive ID today then they'll do an autopsy. We'll have to wait for the medical examiner's recommendations, but given that, I can begin to make appropriate arrangements, funeral arrangements.

He keeps moving his mouth after this, and I try to imagine what else he could be saying. He sneaks a few glances at me, places a hand on my shoulder, pushing me solid into the seat.

I keep nodding in response, but for some reason the folk song about Charlie getting stuck on the train, riding forever beneath the streets of Boston, repeats through my head. Especially the chorus, Will he ever return, no, he'll never return, and his fate is still unlearned, poor Charlie.

I nod because anything Bill might say I can answer yes: Can you do this? It must be hard for you; Are you afraid? It'll be OK; It'll soon be over; Do you wish it'd been different? Do you wish it'd been you?

And then I remember, the song was by the Kingston Trio. I loved this album. The cover, a '60s record, and the singer was wearing a cane hat with a floppy brim, clamdiggers torn at the ankles. It was worn by my fingers, and bent at the edges. I was a child. I didn't take care with anything. I'd put on records and dance and sing, and now I try to laugh, thinking that Bill's Jamaican, but when I open my mouth, nothing at all comes out.

We drive. The only sounds I hear rise from my stomach. I'm hungry, but I like this feeling. It feels appropriate, swimmy and tight. The windows, opaque with rain, the streets stained, spreading. This is a trick I learned recently: my eyes in slits, I relax into silence, relax into dread. And all those games we played, Reese and I, games no one could win.

There were many varieties: all to make me strong, she said.

Closed doors, Reese crushing my head between her knees, threading straight pins, the type with colored heads, through the skin of my neck, my back, piercing the outer layers. Into my thighs, buttocks, too terrified to move, they felt like countless insects pausing across my surfaces: a look of pleasure on Reese's face afterward graciously stroking lotion into the wounds.

There, she'd say. All healed.

She'd place her head to mine, our hair a veil.

Or: Katey, she'd ask. Do you believe in love?

And one time: Your heart's shaped just like a fist, she said. That's why they say it's beating.

Always I was grateful.

Always I closed my eyes, imitating sleep: stationary, subdued, operative.

★

I could tell someone all this, but what does that say about me?

The one time I saw Reese cry, I said, Let's play. She was reluctant, but I tied her where she lay, three times around her wrists and ankles with pantyhose. She sobbed harder and harder. She was powerless and I hated her for it.

I wanted to beat her for her sadness.

I jumped on my bike and pedaled until my legs thumped, up the river.

Even now I hear her, I hear it inside my ears; she calls, over and over again, Save me, save me.

★

Bill pulls into the lot of a building with no windows. An old armory.

All around this area are buildings like this one, all from the Revolutionary War. My fourth and fifth grade classes would take day trips to these buildings, markers commemorating old encampments, marble quarries, and battlegrounds.

Inside it's like an archive, long metal cabinets lining

the wall, each marked with a label and a letter.

Bill seats me in a chair at the entrance. It's not really a waiting room or reception area, just a chair and a *People* magazine. He holds up his hand and disappears into an office.

It's frozen food aisle cold, the lights washing out most colors, and with the echoes, I can overhear everything.

Someone says, Hello Bill, mostly from their nose, and Bill answers something. There's an argument that I don't understand until I hear, She's too young, then, Well, if she's the only family.

I think the other voice is the medical examiner, and I try to imagine what this is going to be like, put a face to this other voice, maybe Peter Lorre, a short, evil-looking man, then I hear them speak again: There were her . . . friends, Bill says, then a sharp laugh, That won't hold up in court if it goes, and I hear, She healthy? and some more talking.

Bill walks by, says he'll be right back, hands me a cup of coffee. I stare into the cup and decide I don't like coffee anymore. I have my last cigarette and flip through the magazine.

A few minutes later Bill returns with a bag, a white prescription bag and hands me two cups. "This is Diazepam. Valium," he says. "It will help."

I'm glad he knows what helps. He watches me take the pill from one cup and drink the water, smiles remotely and places his hands on my shoulders and squeezes before disappearing into the other room again. He leaves me the bottle. I hold the pill under my tongue. It tastes terrible, sharp and chemical, but I like that it's blue. Blue means ten milligrams, and I hook my tongue through the heart-shaped center.

I know about Diazepam and Darvon and Vicodin and Xanax. Our family lived on pills, everybody, not just Reese. Blue pills for nerves, pink capsules for pain, white narcotics, peach for mood. Pills to stay awake, pills to sleep, thyroid pills, antibiotics, anti-spasmodics, amazing tan bottles of expired pills crammed in the bathroom cabinet and the top pantry shelf.

Our mother didn't believe in pain. Each new pill to untangle the stomach, soften the nerves, blunt want, desire, need.

What they cured was what you meant. We swallowed our words with the pills.

This was our mother's love. We each learned a trick, wiping blood from brushed gums, the inside of dry noses on toilet paper, and we'd cry, or crawl, bringing them to our mother. We all did this. Like cats, split birds swinging between their teeth, we'd bring these gifts of ourselves, these offerings. And our mother would offer a gift in return, something from the cabinets, possibly chosen by color, and a cup of water.

All better, she'd say. Like it never happened.

Then she'd look at us so lovingly she couldn't see for what we were, that we were desperate not for the pills, but to participate, to be held like a doll, a pillow, a soft sweater.

At breakfast, our father dispensed medicine to us like he was feeding ducks, his three daughters watching him hunch over a trifle guillotine, reciting the poison control number like the pledge of allegiance.

Bill returns again with a man, whom I assume is the medical examiner. He is small and stooped, something like Peter Lorre, but his face seems not to have features. He nods at me, and I try to respond, but can't. This seems not to bother him, as much as I can tell, and we watch Bill walk across the room, pull the filter and grounds from the top of the coffee maker, roll some of the sludge into napkins, then hand one to me, one to the examiner. He holds one for himself up under his nose.

"Are you ready?" he asks, and I nod.

The hallway smells like a sick combination of everything I can think of, one at a time. They are the smells of a life, of a restaurant dumpster: oil and meat, separated milk, dish water, stale freezer burn, gravy, beer, rotten fruit, then it clarifies to something more human. Blood and scabs, shit, vomit faint on a carpet, semen, gas, and spit, armpits and sweat. I hold the napkin of coffee to my nose, copying the examiner and Bill, but the woody smell seems worse, so I breathe through my mouth. I taste it. I can taste it.

The examiner leads us into a room, then disappears, rolls a table in, covered in a tarp. He dims the florescent lights while Bill fiddles with a tape recorder.

"Can you say your name? Into here," and he taps a small box of dots at the side of the tape recorder. "That's the microphone. Please say your name," and he holds the recorder out and I lean in.

"Katherine Bruscke."

He nods encouragingly at me, then says the date, his

name, and a case number. He nods again at me, then once at the small man who rolls up his lab coat sleeves, puts on a pair of rubber gloves, and whips down the tarp like a game show host, like shaking out a blanket after a picnic.

My body drops, but I'm still standing, the florescent light seems to dim. I'm looking through steam, through cataracts. I'm terribly afraid.

"Do you know this person?" Bill asks. He sounds tiny, accidental.

I try to nod again. I am a pillar of salt.

"For the record, please state her name."

"Reese." My voice sounds funny so I say it again. "Reese Bruscke."

"Your relation to her?"

"My sister."

★

And now: who can I appeal to, any convictions I may have; who will save me? God, a God, maybe, but not here, the God I knew is the God under Reagan, and that God will not sit now with Reese, will not package my shoulders in goodness and unction, won't turn my face towards the sky, to find much more behind the sun. Light rivulets only in my dreams.

The only God I know dangles on a green basement wall at a St. Bartholomew's Thursday church supper, the sign saying that all were welcome. We walked in alone, our parents parking the Buick.

This will be fun, our mother said, see how the others live, making it a joke. As if we'd come to this church for a laugh, as a field trip because I'd never been inside one before.

Our parents parking the Buick, this is years before Reese would total it, and yes: she was lucky to have lived so long, lucky: that night, when I am nine years old, holding Shay's hand. I am trembling, I'd never been to a church, and was afraid. I stopped trembling quickly, disappointed it looked like a rec room, a cellar, that God had a house like our neighbors.

Reese pushed us forward to the table, macaroni and cheese, baked chicken, string beans, through the congregation eating cafeteria-style, towards the food, mashed potatoes, Pepsi cans, with Jesus Christ himself keeping guard over the hot plates and bowls, high on the wall.

Reese forcing us, pinching, through the staring congregation, *All are welcome* the sign said outside, we were welcome, then I heard my father's leather soles behind us, and my mother tapping, and we followed them, a plate, some food, all those eyes.

We were hungry and we ate; we never had enough. Was there ever a family so hungry? We wanted some of everything, all of which we didn't have, or when we did, moved away from. We were poor in many ways. I remember our mother driving on pretend errands, one night, because Reese had a friend over at dinnertime; she was too embarrassed we didn't have enough, so she smiled, carefree, then drove around while we ate. And later, to catch her doing the dishes, touching her finger gingerly to leftovers and sucking the juice.

Then the prayer before that church meal: I closed my eyes and saw nothing, Please, I thought, let Dad find a job. But this was halfhearted, it wasn't what I meant; what I thought was Please, let them stop staring, but when I opened them again, there was the Jesus watching me back with his painted eyes.

We ate that meal. Shay ate all her vegetables, but no one noticed. My father looped an arm around his plate and ate with a fist. I watched Reese, then did the same: picked all the red meat out of the stir fry, marshmallows from the ambrosia salad, because that was the kind of girls we were.

And that is my God, my God of hunger.

There is no exaltation in my hunger.

Even later, again, in our games: I remember hooking my fingers under Reese's back, frantically whispering *light as a feather stiff as a board light as a feather stiff as a board* but as hard as I tried, I couldn't get her one inch off the ground.

★

Bill calls me a taxi; we stand in the rain. He hangs his sportcoat over my head, massages me like a lover; I cry into the lining. The wool sponges up the water; the back of my throat thick with phlegm, the stink of small pets.

"I had no idea," he says, "she was your sister."

I say nothing. The Valium begins to work over me. I listen to Bill and he curses. The taxi cruises by, then backs up into the lot, through puddles, cleanly, a knife sound. I place the jacket into Bill's hands gently. His eyes are alien, shallow. He seems sadder than me.

"You need to call me," he says.

"I'll call you," I say. "I need some time."

"Yes," he says.

I climb into the taxi; he closes the door after me. The window is open halfway; he grips the glass. "You should have told me," he says, and the taxi moves forward then. He lets go as if pushing. I watch him as we pull away, then bend my fingers in a wave, almost as an afterthought.

FIVE

But I remember it wrong, I tell it wrong. I didn't tell this man I'm not sure loves me I was leaving, not then. If I did, I didn't mean it yet, I wanted him to stop me, cry, come with me. I said it when he was asleep, an unfair trick, so I could be angry, and leave. This was the only way not to disappoint myself. I told him later, while he slept, while he jerked with dreams.

You see, the man I'm not sure loves me, I love very much.

I wanted him to love me. I wanted this desperately.

I'd wait in bed, he'd move through the house, doing everything to avoid coming in. I felt stupid sleeping naked. He'd slip into bed when he thought I was asleep, and I'd sit up and watch, or sit up and think.

In the beginning, it was different. He'd hold me down for hours, four, six, until I hurt, I complained and said, We have to eat, and we'd stumble down the streets of Phoenix, Taos, too tired to drive to a restaurant. French,

Mexican, Italian, it didn't matter, nothing had its own taste when you were in love, it all tasted delicious and he'd look at me, lashes bent on his cheek, hand on my knee. Then I could fool myself that this was a man I didn't know, a type I didn't know, that he listened and loved and would never hurt me. But I watched him even then, when he slept, I stroked his eyelids, his eyes beat below them. I stroked his eyelids and he dreamt and I never knew the end had already begun.

His legs in Levis, ironed a crease down the middle. We were in love.

That made it okay; it was the beginning; it moved quickly. He asked me to leave with him, so poor we slept beneath an Italian flag pulled from a dumpster.

Fucking Goombas, he'd say and smile. It was a joke, we were in love. My skin so dry from the space heater and the desert air he'd pour cooking oil in the bathtub with me, saying, You're a pistol, Katey. I'm glad I got you in my trenches.

We'd drink malt liquor, split a forty and huddle together in alleyways, climb up onto rooftops. The sound of him pissing, speaking inaudibly, the streetlights in the stretch fusing with his words, and I'd pretend it didn't matter what he said, that the world was what we were mad at. I'd swallow, try to look like something he could love.

I was quiet, I barely breathed. I peeked around corners to watch him. I did everything I knew to do. I tied cherry stems with my tongue. I let him spit in my ass and slide in.

I tried so hard to belong, to be a belonging. I loved him maybe with madness, that closeness, like with Reese.

I wonder if Reese knew my love: sneaking into her room, holding perfume bottles, the small strangeness of them against my cheek; her velvet peacoat; the baked scent of her pillowcase. I was sure I could understand the pattern, I could find an answer.

If I couldn't love her, could I be her?

And this man: I smelled the shirts in his closet, so many rooms, always the same closet, the same arrangement of shirts, blue to white. I'd gather them all up in my arms.

Once in awhile, I felt like he and I could be good. One time, the waitress brought our appetizer after the meals and we looked at the garlic bread. I leaned the doggie bag between us on the motorcycle, and two people begged spare change, I gave them the garlic bread instead. I knew what to do. It was a moment I was perfect. He turned around and kissed me. I was reeling, dizzy, and the night felt big around us; I kissed him back until I slid perfectly off the seat, hit the concrete half-kneeling, an ankle bent beneath me. I felt nothing other than that kiss, blood rushing to the spots his fingertips pressed on my cheeks.

Are you all right? he asked, bending towards me, holding out his arm, pulling me to, gently, by the shoulder. Are you all right?

Oh yes, I answered. I do this all the time.

★

The taxi seems to pass gently over the roads. The driver says nothing to me, but he hums under his breath. I watch out the windshield; a crucifix slaps against the glass. I finally lean forward and ask, "Don't you need to know where I'm going?"

He checks me in the rearview mirror; his eyes are black and large. He's on the young side; hair advances down the back of his neck. "I figure you tell me sometime," he says. His English is so accented it still sounds Spanish.

I tell him Annika's address automatically, and he cuts a sharp U-turn down Central Avenue, knocking me against the door. "You need to catch a breath, then you tell me. You come from that place. But for me, you look okay," he says.

"Thanks."

"What your name?" he asks.

"My name?"

"Yes. Never mind," he says.

I read his name first, off the ID tacked to the glove box. Juan Partido Junior. "Katherine," I answer.

He looks back into the mirror. "My daughter's *patrona*," he says. "Her saint. Saint Catherine. *De* Siena." He taps the steering wheel. "Is a good name."

"Thank you."

"She cure all badness of the tongue."

"Badness?"

He thinks about that. "Sicknesses. Sickness of the tongue."

I open my mouth and close it. I see the sharp neon of the CVS Drugstore vivid through the rain, and I think of aspirin, chocolate bars, something to place inside my mouth, my stomach, to pull me closer to the ground. A bottle of water for another Valium. "Hey," I say, "can I make a stop?"

He seems not to hear me, but pulls into the lot, up to the fire lane. "The meter runs," he finally answers. He looks sheepish. "I no stop it, but you have for another fifteen bucks. The policeman pay."

"I just need a few things," I say, and he hits the powerlocks. The doors swing open. "Do you want anything?"

The driver tilts his head and smiles into the mirror, his canines gray, dead. He drapes an arm over the passenger's seat, and I jump out of the car, move towards the store lights, wondering if I misunderstood his answer: "Do you want anything?" I ask.

"Mrs. the Saint Catherine." The driver smiles. "Salvation."

⋆

Annika's house rises from the darkness, seems like a Valhalla, an oasis, a hot meal, a clean public restroom, someone who speaks English. I am satisfied to stand back outside her door, completely anesthetized and high, at the same time with a pizza delivery guy leaning on the bell. I smell the pie, like an animal. I am starving, and the pizza smells like a combination of everything I can think of, like life. I am starving. The pizza guy looks at me expectantly. He has a large upper lip and three days' growth, and I say, "The door doesn't close, so the bell probably doesn't work either," but my voice sounds strange and strangled from taking two more Valium. He looks down at the pizza box. I grab his arm and lead him into the kitchen.

Tommy Marvette and Josh and Coil are assembled around a board, shouting over a game of Risk. Annika leans against the counter watching, shoelaces untied, her lipstick waxy, her eye yellow under the light, giving her a bewildered look. They're already drunk, and don't hear us come in.

"I got married," I say. "Come meet my husband." The pizza guy says nothing. They all look up, stand, their chairs pitching outward and the board half over, but the pieces stay like a glued-together jigsaw puzzle.

"Look who the fuck's here," Marvette yells. He looks the same, except maybe he's losing his hair a bit. His forehead angles away more steeply than I remember, but he hugs me full-face into his stomach while the others pay the pizza man, I think, because by the time Marvette releases me, he's gone.

"Where'd my husband go?" I ask, but no one laughs at my joke. I've been patted and waved to and everyone's scrabbling over the pizza box so instead I call "Save me a piece, please."

Josh walks in front of me waving a slice, but I'm too slow for it, too slow, and it's a very red and orange piece of pizza and I'm caught up in watching it. "You want it?" he asks.

I nod—like a child, I realize—but it's too late, so I nod again.

Josh winces his glasses higher up his nose. "Jane Goodall says males make female monkeys masturbate for fruit."

I hear Annika laugh from somewhere. I'm very tired. "Is that how you say hello?"

He balances the slice on my palm, but I suddenly have to lie down, and I walk into the living room. Everybody follows except Coil, everyone files in, and sits around me. The cheese slides off onto the rug. No one notices.

"I want to finish the game. Did you see my skill?" Coil calls from the kitchen door. "Europe was next." No one answers. "Cojones," he says, walking in and shaking his head. "Talk to me about cojones."

Josh wipes his mouth. "I need to tell you?"

"That's what I'm saying." Coil sits down next to him and whistles a few bars of Don Giovanni.

It feels just like high school again. I check my arm where a watch would be.

"Look. We're all together." Annika says finally. She's drinking vodka and Gatorade from a teacup. She offers some to me, and it deadens my tongue, like candied ginger. My throat sucks it up. She smoothes her hair. "Well, almost."

"Except Don," Marvette says. He bounces his leg and looks at me across the couch. "You shouldn't blame yourself."

I place the teacup on the carpet. "Why would I blame myself?"

This is the wrong thing to say. Josh throws his pizza against the wall. No one moves. It sticks two feet up and slides to the molding, the grease dilute as a watercolor.

"He was in love with you," he says. Don was his best friend.

"Bullshit," I say. My tongue is blunt inside my mouth. "He wasn't my type."

Josh stretches out and cracks his bad knee. He isn't looking at me. "Everyone's your type."

I close my eyes and push off the couch arm and Tommy's leg. I get up and make my way to the bathroom, holding on and resting first on a chair, the bookshelves, and then along the walls.

"What's with you?" Annika calls.

I turn and look at her. "Valium." Everything takes a long time, and I feel strangely dramatic, like Tallulah Bankhead. It's quiet for a long moment, and I'm overwhelmed when everyone splits into chatter. "Where did you get that? You see Shay? You didn't get us any? I want a sister who's in pharmacy school. Can I have one? Or two? Or three?" They move towards me. I am having trouble trying to catch up. Tommy hoots, "Rico-Shay."

I hold my hands over my ears. "Shut up, shut up."

Tommy hoots again, then points at me and says evenly, "That's what I missed most about you, Katey. Your sister."

*

I splash my face in Annika's bathroom, catch myself in the cracked mirror, the glass worn away black in places, and watch my face peel away, a pulpy, overripe fruit.

I can see my own brain. Through where my eyes should be, a bruised guava, sweltering and pink. My thoughts swell with brine and gum, the tendrils unknot, covered in fine hairs, swim away from me. Beneath the surface of the mirror, like an ice-caked puddle, I can see it, and everything I've ever known, swimming away from me.

The arch of my jaw, my teeth a picket of tiles, all the same length and very close together. My canines round level to the molars, uncut wisdom teeth nudge like beans out of my gums. I can't scream, cry out, or vomit in the plugged toilet. My tongue lies in my mouth like a shrimp.

Reese breaks through the front door, years ago. It cracks and slams, first the screen, then the door. Our mother holds up her hand, to silence us; we are all eating supper, chicken and peas, iceberg lettuce and carrots. Reese weaves violently through the house, stomping, possessed, she volleys into the dining room, and pushes herself across the table, tossing Shay's plate across the room before falling towards our mother. Reese has something in her mouth, her face and eyes rattled. We sit still and wait, we let her move, there is no expression on my father's face. I stare at my plate. No one else makes a sound; Reese chokes and heaves.

None of us had seen Reese in over a month.

She twists to the carpet, almost fainting, our mother's chair tips back, she looks afraid, but it leans into Reese's torso. She turns her face towards our mother and spits: whatever it is misses her, arcs towards the table. It is a tip of a tongue, and it lands, skates across the wood in blood, and hits the bowl of peas. Reese laughs, blood in her mouth, on her chin in streams. I am relieved—it is not her tongue—but Shay screams, and our father jumps up and shields her, urging her away with his arm. My mother stares at the tip, it is just a scrap really, pithy and firm, like something from the meat section, the blood thinned by saliva. Reese lies onto the floor and rolls back, our mother's chair falls, but she catches herself and stands. I have not moved.

I've blocked the rest out. All I remember is our mother tweezing the tongue between her fake nails, dropping it into the balance of Shay's glass of milk, how it colored and thickened like strawberry ice cream. All I remember is realizing Reese rode the bus forty blocks or so with it between her teeth. That there was something wrong.

I don't know what happened to the tongue. I never asked. I was always told. This is how I learned. Reese told me everything, and I believed.

Lay down to zip tight jeans. If they're really tight, use a bent wire hanger for leverage.

A spot of Ambesol numbs your eyebrows for tweezing. Nine times tables you can figure on your hands. It's possible nothing's what it seems.

You have to be strong.

So, I don't cry out or scream because I don't believe what I see. I'm dreaming and delirious—it's the pills working through me, showing me—my body splitting, this easily, this gladly. At this point, my stomach seizes and I knock a bottle of perfumed talc into the air, sneeze, then throw up in Annika's bathroom sink. The sink is clotted with strange hairs. My nose feels kicked by the acid, the bile. It tastes metallic and sharp. My skin, sunburned. I burn; I have to endure the burning.

I close my eyes against the reflection. When I open them again, I will be beautiful.

★

So, really: it's the same as ever. She is still with me; I can't escape Reese.

No matter where I go, when I walk I watch the ground. There's too many faces, not much different than mine or hers. She follows me like this, and I was afraid to actually see her, afraid she'd recognize me, see me for what, whatever I am.

I failed her. I can't run anymore. And now I can't die.

This thought scares me somehow. That I may wish to die, but cannot. I am harbinger, messenger. I must bear witness.

This is my place, taped to the couch.

I must live. I must live with myself.

I look back into the bathroom mirror. My face has returned, flushed and bluish.

I don't believe what I see, because I know better, but I feel my cheeks just to make sure.

I run the sink to clean out the vomit, and wash my

face with cool water. I look like shit: red-rimmed and puffy. None of the boys I knew ever told me I was pretty until later, told me straight out. I dressed to hide my body, stovepipe jeans to balance my thighs, chunky shoes for my tiny ankles. Long-sleeved shirts that covered the waist, but dipped low at the neck.

Don. Now I am thinking of Don. Donald Horvath. Levitt. Donald Levitt Horvath. There was a commercial, furniture discount, a woman singing on the TV, You'll love it at Levitt's, and how Don smiled. He once bought me a ski hat for a birthday, lined with Thinsulate. I was sixteen then, seventeen, up on Annika's Beamer drinking whiskey and Thera-Flu in the library parking lot. Celebrating, I called it. He turned the hat inside out, pointing out its features. Warm to negative seventy. And a zine. You'd like this, he said. *ANSWER Me!*, that's what it was called. He ordered it from *Factsheet Five* when they were first starting out. He politely turned the pages for me, bold line drawings of rape, children without arms, the complete oil paintings of John Wayne Gacy. He saw something in me that wasn't there. He painted an image over my face.

I must have talked to him again after that, but in my mind, this is the last time.

Don, he went to Earlham College, supposed to graduate 1995. He dropped out, I heard, converted to the Quakers. He became a Quaker missionary to the Sandinistas, to-be class of 1995, groping around in the jungle, braided with age.

And then he died.

When it happened, I didn't think much of it. I didn't think much of him when he was alive, anyway. I couldn't love him. I'd never return his calls, sit next to him, the way he whistled through his nose. If he loved me, I didn't notice. He was everywhere, the periphery, his laugh too long, too loud. I didn't understand much, the rumors, a tropical disease, political prisoner. I didn't think I was afraid of death, and it happened so far away. His parents cremated him there. It was just a phone call. Where I was, New Mexico, Baja, I don't remember. Annika found me, called our parents for my phone number.

It was a curiosity, an excuse to find me.

Don's died, Annika said, Did you hear? And I hadn't.

Then she said, They're burning him.

I didn't think I was afraid of fire.

But our oldest sister slept, when she slept, with the lights on before I knew to be afraid of anything. I follow her example. Today, I think of Donny and I am afraid.

⋆

Except my man with the motorcycle. He told me everything else, all the things Reese left out. And I believed him.

He was a friend, a friend-of-a-friend, a friend-of-a-friend's brother: temporarily in town and out of money, or something like that. I could never tell, strictly speaking, where he'd come from. I licked his hand and pushed it into the flame; this is how we met. He said he loved me that moment. I was at a party, he was drunk, sprawled on the couch clicking a Zippo.

See, I said. It doesn't hurt like this.

He told me later my eyes came forward and all he wanted to do was kiss me. The party moved above us; we watched it like weather.

Then he was sleeping floor to floor, sororities mostly. I liked him, at first for no reason. He barely spoke. Then I liked him because he'd speak to me.

That's the life, he said. Sugar mommas. Find me a woman to take care of me.

I had to think about that. And he could get one, he could: a pretty boy, brown eyes, an orderly face. But it wasn't what he wanted. He wanted to take care of. Somehow he ended up sleeping on my floor one night.

You're just whoring yourself out, I answered.

He bit his lip. It wasn't the answer he was looking for.

Let's go swimming, he said.

We went up to the reservoir. We stared out over the pool, he talked about his travels, I told him of mine, here to there. That I'd never been any place besides my hometown and then there, that I woke up the 11:15 nonstop one-way to Denver screaming out of a nightmare; the paper pillow jacket soaking wet, my arms wedged wrongways in my sweatshirt. That everything I owned sat in the abs of that plane. How my reflection was caught between the doubled plexiglas, bleary and confused, and I thought vaguely of dyeing my hair.

I'm glad you didn't, he said. Dye your hair.

I liked him, the way he nodded, and that his eyebrows met in the middle.

He asked me about my classes.

They're OK, I answered.

You don't sound sure, he said.

Sure of what? I asked back, and he laughed.

Have you ever seen the ocean? he asked then, and I said, Sure, of course.

He looked at me and I held in my stomach and looked back out at two boogie boarders flat and distant in the background. A wave machine jiggled the lake water over to the shore.

You should see the desert, he said.

Isn't this? I asked.

He shook his head. Not the real one. There, the horizon, he said, the way it wraps around you, and he moved his arms to demonstrate. I nodded. In the desert, he continued, it's bigger, and the stars are as big as your fist. Night rings the world, and the only things that live are the rocks. The rocks, he continued, flicker with the stars, exercising off their glut of the sun. The only sea's the sky. He fully turned to me. As warm as you.

I felt myself rise a bit; Don't you want to see that? he asked, looking at my lips, It's magic.

The ocean's beautiful too, I whispered, startled.

He grabbed my hand, You are beautiful, he said.

I shook my head, My legs, I said and pointed down at them, I'm a pastry. And, I continued, I'm filled with sand. I brushed the bottom of my suit.

He laughed. You, he answered. Make me a pearl.

★

Someone's put on the Pixies. "Doolittle", loud. Everyone is dancing. I weave through them and flop back onto the couch. Annika poses in front of me, then stops, holds her hands out to me. "Dance with me, Katey," she yells over the music.

I laugh. She's lost one shoe, but doesn't seem to notice. Coil has a lavender boa wrapped around his neck, the ends squirm through the air like muppet arms. The boa's left over from some Hallowe'en, I surmise, and Coil and Josh are tumbling a tango back and forth into the kitchen. It's a grotesque scene. They look something like zombies.

"Come on," Annika calls. "I'm waiting."

I shake my head in protest. "I can't dance."

Annika straddles me and pushes me back into the pillows. "You can dance," she says. "I've seen you."

I shake my head again. Everything looks blurry. "I can't stand up." Annika waves, then rolls off me and dances towards Josh and Coil, who have separated and look like they're trying to breakdance. Marvette comes over and sits next to me. He hugs me again, enthusiastically, then leaves his arm around my shoulders. His plaid shirt is wool or something, it smells like dog and feels gritty against my neck. "Katey," he says. "Good to see you." He pokes a finger from his free hand into my belly. "Katey."

I smile at him, but my vision's getting worse; colors are fusing now, their separations vague, planes flattening.

"I have no depth perception," I say.

He laughs at that. I don't think it's funny; I'm starting to feel nauseated again. He leans back and crosses his legs. "So what's new with you, Katey?" he asks.

"Lately?"

"Sure."

"In my life?" I'm impatient.

He smiles blankly. "How about today? What happened to you today?"

"I got off the Greyhound. I came here. That's it." I put my hand on my forehead. I feel hot. "And I saw Squid."

Marvette sits straight and looks at me. His mouth is open; I can tell because all I see is black. "You saw Squid?"

I nod.

"Christopher Dochovny?"

I nod again. "Yes. Squid. I forgot."

Marvette gets up off the couch to turn down the music. "Katey here saw Squid. Today," he says to everyone else. "She forgot."

I hear Josh's voice across the room. "You forgot?"

"This morning," I say. "In front of the bus terminal. He mugged me."

"You forgot?" Josh calls again.

I nod again. Then I hear Coil. "Christopher Anchovy."

"Squid Anchovy," Josh corrects. Then I hear them slap each other five.

"She forgets the captain of the fucking swim team mugs her," Coil says.

And Annika. "He mugged you?"

Then Josh again. "He's not the captain anymore, thank you."

Coil snickers at that. "That's 'cause," he says, "we're not in high school anymore."

Annika: "Oh yeah?" to him, then, "He mugged you?" to me.

Marvette sits back down next to me. He washes in and out of focus. "What happened?"

"I got off the bus. He mugged me. That's it. Someone grabbed my arms and said, 'Scream and I waste you'."

Josh: "Is that a quote?"

I ignore him. "And it was Squid."

"He had a gun?" Annika asks.

"So what happened then?" Marvette asks.

"We went to a coffee shop. I ate melon, he had a danish."

Annika waves her arms up and down. "That's who you ate with?"

"I always hated him." Josh says.

"Holy shit," Marvette says. "How'd he look?"

I get a cramp in my stomach. "He's a junkie."

Annika stands behind me and places her chin on the top of my head. "How could you forget all this?"

"I had other things on my mind," I say.

She lifts her head and moves away. "And that's it?"

I hear Coil laugh. "He's a junkie?"

"I had other things on my mind," I repeat.

"Did he give you the Valium?" Josh asks.

I hug myself and lean over. "Shut up about the Valium already."

No one says anything for a bit. Josh finally turns back up the Pixies. Marvette empties the last of his beer, grabs my arms and pulls me up, close to him. "Let's dance," he says. He holds me close, my chin rests on his shoulder, and we slow dance; he rocks his hips, I stand stiffly, my guts roll from the inside.

The worst nausea is from not having eaten anything. My stomach heaves acid and air, but Tommy Marvette grips me tightly, sings in my ear. *Cease to exist, giving my goodbye . . .*

"Excuse me," I say. He presses into me and we barely move. It takes most of my strength to shake his arms off me. I sink down to the floor. "I have to go."

He watches me crawl across to the bathroom. He sings *You'll think I'm dead, but I sail away, on a wave of mutilation, wave of mutilation, wave of . . .* He sings after me, watching me crawl.

*

I'm startled when Annika knocks at the door. "Katey?" she calls. "Hello?"

She knocks twice more, then more persistently. "I'm coming in," she threatens, then pushes the door open. I'm sitting under the sink, the floor still downy with the spilt talcum powder. She stands in the doorway, Marvette behind her wearing one of my bras on the outside of his shirt. Someone's changed the CD to Superchunk, Josh screaming along. Marvette shakes my pack at me, it's open, and socks fall out, rolled jeans, a stick of deodorant. The bra is my favorite, a mesh one, underwire, black, somewhat sexy except the underpants disappeared long ago. The bra's elastic digs into his soft middle, tight like a string. The cups flap and hang, desiccated. "Hey. Maybe what I missed most," he declares, "is you."

Annika steps in, slams the door quickly in Marvette's face. I can still hear his laughter. She squats down next to me. "Hey," she says.

Her voice is gentle and stern, as if she's caught me eating paste. This is the first time I can see her as a teacher, except her eye is a darker mustard-yellow and swollen. Her lipstick's completely worn off, except in the corners, and there's a rip in her tights. I'm in range of her breath, spiny with vodka, severe.

She holds onto the sink with one hand, and pokes my neck gently with the other. "You're getting a rash, right there." She ducks under a bit more and scrutinizes it, closing one eye; she looks like she's aiming at me. "Little red dots."

I still don't answer. I'm not sure I can.

"So," she says. "You gonna tell me what the fuck is going on?"

I sit back and breathe.

"You said you had other things on your mind. Come on," she says. "You're missing the party."

She tries to smile, offers me an arm, as if she were asking me to waltz. I look at it, then back up at her. I don't feel like dancing. She sighs. Defeated, she shakes what she can reach, my knee, and my head hits back against the sink, softly. "Are you pregnant?"

I almost laugh. I am far from that. I carry no news of life, but of death. Annika squats back, leaning off her foot. She said the nail bed still hurt always, as if something were trying to break through. I can feel this, as if it were, right now, my own. "Let me." I clear my throat. "Let me," I begin. "Let me see your foot."

★

I don't sleep, Reese would say. Maybe it's because I have no dreams.

These are the things my sister would tell me in the night, burrowing into bed with me.

Do you know what heroin is? she asked one time, rolling towards me. Do you know what that is yet?

I hid my face in my pillow. I didn't know how to answer. I thought of Wonder Woman, her thigh-high boots and golden lasso, and of blonde Betty and Veronica, high school trysts with Archie, bouncy hair, glamour. I thought of Emma Peel and the Mod Squad. I thought of Reese breathing quietly next to me.

Sure, I said insistently, of course.

I thought my sister taught me everything, but there are things I've come to understand on my own.

I don't believe her. She had dreams.

This is what I know: Reese was afraid of the dark.

I am dreaming.

"Can you hold your arms above your head?"

"Where am I?" I ask. It's dark. I'm sitting up.

"Hold your arms, Katey." Annika says. She reaches over and clicks on the nightstand lamp. "You need to sleep."

I blink at the light. The clock next to it is flashing 12:00. "Have I been sleeping?"

I look around. I'm on a mattress in the middle of a room. The walls are flimsy, painted matzo, discolorations the shape of tools. Water drips travel down lengths of twine, thumb-tacked to the ceiling, down into pots and pans across the floor.

Annika stands over me, drags my shirt over my head and throws it into a corner. "You passed out," she says. "You don't remember?"

"How could I remember if I was passed out?" I point at the pans. "What is this, a yard sale?"

She doesn't answer that, but places something soft across my lap. "Put this on," she says. "It's raining."

I drop the nightgown on; it's satin, cold and slippery like dish soap.

"Don't puke on it." She clicks off the lamp. "Good night."

★

There are the moments when I don't know who I am, I can't remember anything about myself, and can't believe I am real. I look at my body, down at my arms, my breasts bulging outward under a sweater I can't remember buying. I look around at my things that I am amazed belong to me. I've wandered into a stranger's house, her frame, I've walked into the wrong hotel room. I'm aware and puzzled, conscious, and it doesn't help to say my name; it sounds removed and arbitrary. I could easily be someone else, but I'm not, I don't think.

Those moments are dim: a light snaps off and I listen to my breath, this attention keeping me alive.

★

I feel the breath on my face before I hear the "Katey," said urgently, as if they were about to give up, but not before trying again, begging "Katey, Katey. Katey, it's me." They pull me awake. This is a voice I have waited for.

"Hi, Shay," I answer.

Shay lets out a long sound from the back of her throat. I can't see her and can't tell if it's still dark in the room or if my eyes are closed. "How do you feel?" she asks.

I sit up. The nightgown is twisted up around my neck and I'm glad for a second the lights are off. My mouth is dry. "Fine," I say. "And you?"

She knocks the lamp over, then rights it on the ground and turns it on. I pull the sheet over my chest. "They called me," she says.

She looks good. Her hair's longer than I remember, and loose, clinging with static like spider webs to her black sweater. She's put in some red highlights. "Annika says you wouldn't wake up."

"Yeah?" I say.

She covers her face with her hands and sits for a minute. Her hair falls across her face. "Yeah," she finally says. "Where are your clothes?"

I point to where Annika threw my shirt. She gathers up my top and shoes and places them on my lap. "They didn't know what to do. They called me."

"So?"

Shay eases towards me and leans in. She reaches out softly and tugs down the skin of my lower lids, studies my eyes. "Do I have to take you to the ER?" She pulls away and I shake my head. "You wouldn't wake up."

I shake my head again and look down at my clothes.

"So, I don't know," she continues, helplessly. "They called me. They're stupid. Who knows? They're your friends." She's silent for a minute, then says, "Get dressed. I'm getting your stuff."

Shay walks out, then returns with my backpack. "This is it?" she asks. Setting it down, all business, she shuffles through it, pulls out a book, looks at the title, puts it back in, and finds the Diazepam. "Ten milligrams?" She shakes the bottle at me. "How many of these did you take?"

"I don't know," I say, pulling on my shirt.

She raises an eyebrow and opens the bottle. "Where did you get these? Who's this doctor?"

"My head hurts."

"No shit." She drains the bottle into her hand and counts the pills. "Were you trying to kill yourself?"

"I don't know, Shay. Maybe."

She paces the room. "You wouldn't wake up," she hisses. "What's the matter with you?"

"I blacked out." I stand up slowly and step into my boots.

"Do you remember anything from yesterday?"

"Reese," I say.

Shay stops moving and looks at me. "Huh?" Her hair has grown, it shreds and falls.

"Nothing," I say. "I was just thinking you look like Reese in this light." I feel like crying.

"Like Reese?" she repeats.

"Can we go home?" I ask, softly.

"Not like this," she says, standing up. "Not right now." She puts my pack over one arm. "But let's get out of here."

I hear a cough and the door opens.

"Want me to carry you?" Danny asks.

"No," I say. "Thanks, Danny."

Shay raises another eyebrow at me. I shrug and Danny moves forward and presses his shoulder into my stomach and lifts me like a two by four. He carries me out through the living room, and Shay follows. Annika and Josh sit on the couch and watch us leave. I hold up my head and look back at them for as long as I can. We're off the porch, across the yard, almost out to Shay's Celica when I remember to wave goodbye, almost as an afterthought.

SIX

I wake up staring at a ceiling mural of the Periodic Table of the Elements.

The toilet flushes, once, twice, and Shay emerges in a plaid robe.

"Sexy," I say.

"Well," Shay says. She tightens the sash. "I mean, it's only you."

"Thanks." I sit up and point at the ceiling. "How'd I miss that?"

"You were DOA." She walks into the kitchen and returns with a glass of orange juice in an old spaghetti sauce jar. "Like my place?" she asks, handing it to me. "I call it the 'Midwestern Dorm' look. Cement block, inflatable, second-hand and covered with a bedsheet." She perches on the edge of her bed, and I look at her back, clavicles hooking through the flannel, shoulders curved like parentheses. "How do you feel?"

"Fine, thanks," I say, finishing the juice. "And you?"

She looks down at her legs under the robe. "You want toast? I'll make some toast." She gets up and moves towards the kitchen again, but stops and turns to me. "I didn't know you snored," she says. "You snore."

I don't know what to say to that. "You've never seen me sleep."

Shay lies on her stomach, her face three inches from the inner binding of a book. Her eyes don't seem to move across the page at all, and she finally slams it and groans. I'm cross-legged on the carpet, arms to elbows deep in my backpack pulling out clothes. Shay rolls over, and watches me. "You look like you're birthing calves."

"Nothing to wear," I answer. "Everything is dirty."

"You want something to eat?" Shay asks me. "You only have like, two days of clothes in there."

"No."

"Some more juice?"

"No," I say. "No thanks."

She sits up. "So," she says. "How are you?"

"Fine." I dump the contents of my pack onto the floor and frown, pull my toothbrush from inside my pack and smell it.

"Katey. Eat something already. I made toast."

"What were you reading?" I ask.

"Organic chemistry."

"Wow," I say. I unroll a pair of jeans that look vaguely clean and check the crotch on them to make sure. "Everything smells."

Shay tightens her lips. "Wear something of mine. We're sisters."

I carefully pile my clothes. "That we are."

She gets up and moves towards her closet. "Here." She pulls a denim shirt from a hanger, smiles, and tosses it at me. "This is extra large like you wear. You like it?"

"Thanks." I shrug and place it on top of my jeans. "Sure."

She stares into the closet silently; I roll my clothes back into my backpack, arranging them to fit. I realize how little I did take, that when it comes down to what I think I need, really need, it isn't much at all, that I could live out of this pack, and it isn't that heavy at all, and I'm thinking about this, and what I left behind. I try to see myself as swift, sure of destination, carrying only the essentials, but again, the truth is I agonized, packing in front of the air conditioner. I just couldn't tell what was important besides two days of clothes, the next two days.

Suddenly I hear ripping, jangling metal, seams from the other side of the room.

Shay has broken. She is angry with me. She tears down all her clothes and throws them around, some at the floor, but mostly at me. I have no time to react. She screams, "Fuck you!" at me, but her voice sounds cut, like she's screaming through a fan, running towards me with an armful of garments, blues, greens, florals.

"Here, fuck you. Take what you want." She drops them on my head, burying me, the smell of soap and some perfume, musky. Then she swings at me, bats at my shoulders and whatever she can reach. "But there is nothing you want." I grab at her, punching free, and we wrestle; she screams "Fuck you!" over and over again at me, into some kind of crescendo, "We're sisters, we're sisters."

I find her knees and pull, she rams her foot into my backpack accidentally, then trips over me and falls onto her back, panting, kicking her legs like a beetle. She's crying.

I watch her for a second and catch my breath, she seems conquered and lies still. There are clothes, hers, mine, hanging everywhere. "What's your problem?" I ask.

"We're sisters," she sniffles. Her face is red, her eyes small and strange.

"I know that," I say. "I know."

It's obvious she thinks I don't understand, and she rolls helplessly over onto a pillow of sweaters and buries her face. Her shoulders flutter soundlessly. "You don't have to talk to me," she says, muffled.

But I do understand. She doesn't want the truth any more than I do. The truth pushes like an illness; it is no mystery why our little sister is a pharmacist. "Well," I say. "Don't cry."

She says nothing, doesn't move, doesn't believe me. I reach over, spilling a pyre of shirts, tug the cardigan away from her face.

"Hello," I try, gently, forcing a smile. "Hello in there." I sound like I'm addressing a dog. "It's OK." She sobs harder. I rub her back, the skin stretched across her like pantyhose.

"Jesus, Shay, OK. What do you want to know?"

This makes her sit upright and I hand her a sock I recognize. "Here," I say. "It's clean."

She blows her nose into it, swabs her eyes. "What has happened, Katey? What was yesterday? I want to know what's going on."

"Ask me."

"What's going on?"

I finally say, "It's not that easy." She studies me, looks for a sign I'm lying, of weakness. I straighten up my face.

"Where you know Danny from?"

I bite my lip. "I don't."

Shay raises her eyebrows a few times. "You knew Danny. You said his name last night. When we picked you up." She waits patiently for my answer, chews a few strands of hair. I clench at the grainy, dry sound.

"Did I?"

"He said you were over here yesterday."

I look at the floor.

"He fucks everybody, Katey. He fucks everybody."

"So do I."

I play with the buttons on a pair of Shay's shorts, flung atop of a pile.

"What about, you know?" she asks.

I sigh, get the zipper stuck. "I don't want to talk about him."

"He called here too. Yesterday. Left a message. Then he called again. Said you took off."

"Oh yeah?" I ask.

"I said I hadn't seen you." She sighs, looks serious. "I hadn't. Did you break up? Is that it?"

"What it?"

Shay grabs the shorts from me. "You took six Valium."

"That's not going to kill me." I place my head in my hands.

"Oh God, my poor sister," Shay cries. "A broken heart."

We lie back onto the clothes. "So, what do you call this look?" I ask. "Exploded dryer?"

She laughs, then we're quiet. I stare up at the mural. It has to be eight feet wide, six feet tall. Shay's apartment isn't that large. I read down the last list, He, Ne, Ar, Kr, Xe, Rn. "What's those again?"

"Noble gases."

"Noble gases. Right. I'd really like a cigarette," I say.

Shay jumps up, brushes herself off. "Hold on a minute." I hear a drawer open, then something glass pulled from a shelf. She sits down next to me, puts two cigarettes in her mouth, lights them, then places one between my lips.

"You smoke?"

"No," Shay says, inhaling.

We are a still life, the two of us, sisters, strangers, the sun low across our laps like bars, cigarette smoke pillowing like fog on a ribbon. A pastel, soft and muddled around the edges, blending into the mess.

But we are not paper, printed on only one side.

"I'll be OK now," I say. I think I'm lying.

"You saved me," I add. This I mean.

Shay holds up her hands. "You can only save yourself." I button up Shay's denim shirt. She watches me. "I have some triamcinolone acetonide for that rash. It's a common side effect to a Diazepam overdose."

"I'm glad we talked," she says. She strokes my cheeks, then pulls me towards her, hugs me, kisses my forehead.

"I'm glad you're here, whatever the reason."

"I'll be at school, then the pharmacy all day." Shay dresses efficiently, picking from the floor by color, peacock blue sweater, hooks a bra underneath, jeans, a scarf, sifting through a dish on her dresser for a barrette, clips in, checks the mirror. A pair of my underwear dangle from a knob. She rubs some Vaseline on her lips, eyelids, pulls a leather jacket from under the bed, zips her bag. "Don't clean up, rest. Read. Play Nintendo. Mom wants us for dinner."

"You spoke to Mom?"

"I speak to her every day."

"What'd she say?" I ask.

"She said 'Katherine? My other daughter Katherine?' She said your name in three syllables."

"Shit."

"She said, 'So what? Did someone die?'"

★

Time always moved over our family, moving over us silently.

We gathered dust, we lived like bordering countries. Everyday events secret; there was no common language to use.

If I said, I'm afraid. I'm confused, our mother would clutch her sides, answering, Oh darling, my arthritis. Lupus. Fibromyalgia.

Our father falling silent, waiting to be excused.

It couldn't be what I meant.

That's not what I meant, I'd say. It's okay. I'm fine.

I'd kill my words, and in killing them, slowly die. This is what I learn from Reese. All the games.

To make me strong, she said.

If I'm strong, then they will love me.

Reese crying. I double knot the hose; she opens her mouth and closes it again. She is caught. I am hunting her pain. She tells me everything but her pain.

We know nothing of pain.

Nights moving through our parents' house, picking up, putting down: I smell every object, hold it to my cheek. I riffle through the garbage can. Lights through the window, but not on the street. When I walk, I watch the ground.

1991. The last time I see Reese alive. I reach for her. She pulls away, backs up without looking.

M staring out into the distance. Look, he says, pointing. Look out there.

And now, the dead move again.

And time moves, without warning. In a moment, everything's different. In a moment, we are no longer the people in the photographs. Time misses any documentation between these moments, and these connections.

Never mind, I say. It's all going to be fine. You're the best. Look how close we are. We have each other. We have all these things. How wonderful. What more could I want.

I smile. I try to remember what I was thinking. I shut my mouth.

Silence is the only lie.
Forward is where I am going to. I carry little with me.
Lying is easy. I come from a place of lies.

So, in time we moved prepositionally: over, around, near, beside. Away.

★

These are some of the things in Shay's apartment.

One couch, tweed, veiled loosely by a bedsheet, printed with cowboys and lassoes, gray spurs.

A dresser from our parents' house, white particleboard and Formica. We each had one.

Two posters, one of Tom Waits. A bulletin board, a class schedule, a ticketstub from the 8:05 showing of *The Piano*, a calendar of quotable women, exactly one year out of date.

Black metal garage shelves: books arranged in alphabetical order by title, by subject, by cover, hard to soft.

One lava lamp, one pile of mail: phone bill, Visa bill. Three catalogues: a mountaineering shop, another filled with items of interest to NPR listeners, *Victoria's Secret*. Nothing is circled.

A bottle of Advil, a packet of Clearasil. Baby shampoo, three bars of Zest, toothpaste for tartar, a cube of rock-candied mineral salts, lavender essential oil.

One boar bristle hair brush, rosewood handle, varnish sanded down in fingertip spots.

Three hairs behind the sink.

Ice tea mix, giant red kidney beans, cinnamon. A tomato, apple juice, ginger ale. One lime. Unsalted butter, two packages of turkey bacon and a six-pack.

I unwrap the bacon, find a pan, and turn it on a low flame. I stare at the beer.

"For what we've been through," I say, jamming the cap on the counter edge, pop it open, and hold it aloft like a torch, in a toast.

Gathering the scattered clothes, I begin to sort and fold: one stack of T-shirts. It seems like the least I can do.

One crate of bras and underpants. White cotton, pink cotton, and blue satin.

One cardboard hatbox. Birthday cards from our mother, a high school tassel, six report cards marked *excellent, stupendous, A+*, a single earring, two photos of a boy I don't know, one love letter, one break up note, two W-2s. Postcards from me. *Ay Shay, saw the Grand Canyon; School's fine; I'm taking time off; Money's tight; Happy Easter; Ha Ha; Hope alls well; See you soon; SWAK; K.*

Two jackets: a nylon windbreaker and a wool duffel. One white lab coat. Nike crosstrainers, patent pumps, worn brown Doc Marten boots. Three rayon dresses, ten pairs of blue jeans, one pair of black, and a dozen sweaters on hangers.

I've lived with her most of my life, yet she remains

distant, vicarious, like a celebrity whose face I've painstakingly memorized, both completely familiar and unattainable, and all I know firsthand are of their past roles and fragments of gossip. Even my postcards to her are distant as a fan letter. And her apartment a museum, her possessions alien in their cleanliness, their practicality, even their presence. Objects that assemble our little sister: a shrine, everything I don't know. These are the things she worked for, picked out herself.

And again, her things: arcane symbols marking presence, marking history, temporary, but insistent. I think of psychometrists, psychics reading vibrations from watches, earrings, neckties; they can tell you the owner's dreams, most secret desires, even their blood type.

I have none of this. I could disappear without a trace.

If I had a place to go. Forward. Forward is where I must go.

I think of myself again, smart, sure of destination, striding through airports, train stations, moving without question towards something. Always moving, but the truth is, I have what I can carry. What I have is what I can see. When I move, I let myself be led. If I could understand the pattern.

The truth is I'm a coward. I am led; I hold out my hands to be taken.

The bacon smokes through the room like dry ice. I gather Shay's clothes together in my arms and inhale. Tide, perfume, drycleaners.

"I should tell her," I say out loud. "They'll get all stretched out this way." I let the clothes swing back from my hands. "Shay, you should never hang up your sweaters."

★

But I'm running out of time. By now, I'm sure Bill's uncovered everything about our family. He's read Reese's records. He knows there are parents a few miles away, a younger sister. He's wondering why. He's wondering about me. What I haven't told him. How I could lie. Why I did this myself.

There are no good answers. I'm supposed to call him, but I can't seem to make myself pick up the telephone.

Of all the bad things I've done, not telling my family is the worst.

I knock over the third empty beer bottle. Outside, the roll of dumpsters. It is Thursday. Shay's clock reads 12 noon.

Maybe Bill's at lunch, exactly 12 to 1, a squat burger joint where they have his coffee ready, a reuben sandwich. Or it's Bill's day off, home with his family, doing whatever people do on Thursday mornings. He's kissed his children to the schoolbus, or maybe he's playing golf, or following his wife through the mall, sighing through another shoe store. Maybe he's not thinking of me at all, of any of this.

I can't think of anything else, how I wept, leaving

cloudy spots on his wool blazer as he called me a taxicab.

I realize I'm holding a plate, not remembering serving the bacon or choosing to eat it.

Moments like these, and I don't know who I am, how I came to be.

How none of my keys seem to fit the first time I try them. Each key left from the apartment before.

And that the garbage trucks bang a song from the cans, a song that filters through the gas to where I stand in my underpants and a borrowed shirt staring into Shay's refrigerator.

But no matter how hard I look in there, nothing new appears.

★

The layout of my hometown is different than the newer suburbs, separated into divisions that circle around one another like lions. My hometown settles down to the river, and you can't get lost here, no matter how hard you try. Through the back lots and alleys, the houses stand uneasily on their foundations, like old photos of Soviet matrons on bread lines. As I walk closer to the water, the fog deepens to gauze. The entire town seems frozen in a nightmare, but it could be I'm making that part up. It becomes difficult to tell where I am, but walking feels good, the cold air.

The bike path thins asphalt to gravel, then into a

creamy primordial mud liquefying to the river. Here it splits into streams, some no thicker than an arm, carving crazily inland, some flowing, others forming puddles and ponds. Trees mature into one another like Siamese twins, a canopy trapping the smell of wet and hair, metallic rotting fruits, crabgrass and wild onions.

It's a good half mile to the Swing; once by the river, it's a half mile from any point in my hometown. It's a torpid pond fed by one of the larger creeks. A cairn of rocks that dams and halts the water's entry.

There are many stories about the Swing. It used to be where you took a date, the unofficial speakeasy, legendary garage band concerts. The swing itself isn't much, a jute rope tied to a maple branch leaning out over the pool. The rope has a few knots in it; the intent was to pull it back, climb the tree, waxy with sap, and jump out. The challenge was to know when to let go, how to land. The pond itself is maybe five feet at its deepest.

The stories are about boys impaled on rocks, broken necks, hangings with the rope itself. Others tell about the parts of dogs and cats and someone's missing potbellied pig, but either way, when I was young, cops began to patrol the area, and before long, the Swing was mostly forgotten.

I make my way into the clearing. It's an ominous place, the pond a dirty suspension, thick as blood. I can't decide if I meant to end up here, across the overgrown path, trying to guess where to stand, sinking into the mud.

I find a root and sit. Everything is still and the

canopy monitors the sunlight down so it feels close to midnight.

What really happened was: he snored into a pillow.

Nights, with my fingers I traced each line, each hair, the moles solid as tablets, memorizing to the point I feel like I've made him up.

This man I'm not sure loves me says I'm only hurting myself. He tells me of my options, his dreams for me and I smile, but when I close my eyes all I can see is what I have.

But what I mean to say is: Up all night, smoking cigarettes there, in the dark, one after the other, until it hurt to lie down, thinking of my sister. He slept blissfully, loose. My nose began to bleed. I listened to him breathe until I couldn't stand it. How easy to hold him there, to kill him, but instead I crept into the bathroom. I pinched my nose and watched the floor.

I closed my eyes against the florescent light. And I realized I'd lost her. I couldn't see her anymore. She was never coming back.

I packed a backpack and slipped back into bed. Goodbye, I said. Goodbye.

★

I carried little with me.

I learned what I could from her. I listened.

Reese left nothing behind. No effects, but affects.

Chewing the inside of her cheeks, covering her face with a hand, her thick brow creased.

I know we all looked alike, but the subtle differences are now gone.

Those blurry snapshots. Sometimes you know a face so well you take it for granted.

Love, I think, is in the details. And I cling to each one. I'm haunted by them.

And the truth is, yesterday, I never got past her hands. Puffed and unripe, studded with blisters, nails separating from the fingers, tense and flat, fixed across her gut.

The white walls set with brushed steel panels. I laid my hand across Reese's.

So, of my options, my dreams: all I have is what I remember.

★

It's too cold for birds or squirrels, but there's movement across the black water. The swing flaps with the wind, itself a sucking inward rush, even though I can't actually feel it blow.

"Katey Bruscke," I hear behind me. It is a voice I recognize. "Are you following me?"

It's Squid's voice. I turn around and try to think of something to say. He moves from behind the tree. He's shirtless, wrapped in a brown wool blanket.

"Hi," I say, surprised.

He flicks the butt of a cigarette over me. It lands in the soft mud and hisses. "Good fucking lord," he mutters, then louder, "Good. Follow me." I half-stand, but he motions and I sit back down again, and he walks beside me.

"What are you doing here?" I ask.

Squid wraps the blanket tightly around him and thinks. "You are following me."

"No," I say.

"Shhh. And they followed you. They're already here." He smiles strangely and points at the trees. "I can see them. Shapes. So I'm waiting," he says and looks proud, like he just finished reciting a difficult poem in front of a class, and sits down. He hasn't shaved since I saw him last, and his chest looks mangy, the ribs like a drying rack. I stare at the fresh bruises and goosebumps. He reaches to touch my arm, carefully, as if it's hot. "You're OK, though. You can be here."

"Oh," I say. "Thanks," which isn't an answer, but I don't know what else to say. "Thanks."

He stands up and moves towards the pond, his back to me, doubled over, laughing at me. Then I realize he's vomiting into the water. The sound is like sugar poured from a canister.

Squid wipes his face with the blanket and sits next to me. He stares out in front of him. Small muscles in his jaw pulse. He watches the pond so deeply, I can't tell what he's seeing. "Will you help me?"

"Of course." That also isn't an answer, but there doesn't seem to be anything else.

"I'm dying," he says into the wind.

"You're not dying."

"Katey," he says. "Look at me. This is what it is to die." He shakes and continues. "It doesn't matter what you think. Inside to out." He grabs my shirt. "Save me."

I nod.

"Save me," he says again, pleading. "Save me."

"Yes," I say. "OK."

He leans into my shoulder, and stretches out an arm. He motions towards the pond. "This," he says. "This is nice, isn't it?"

Squid sleeps sitting up, lulling, then drops towards me, his head settling into my lap like a melon. I reach and unwrap a small bundle by his feet. I expect to see some works, but there's no needles, no spoon, nothing but a roll of bills, all small denominations in a rubber band, the Beretta, a phone card for a Miss Natalie Pashelle, a pack of gum, and some cigarettes. I take five twenties and a cigarette, but can't find a lighter, no matches. His shirt is nowhere to be found. I feel towards his pants pockets, but then stop, so I sit there with the cigarette between my lips.

His face in sleep is jowly and gray like an old man's. He's tensed up, carved from one piece, like a toppled lawn ornament. I giggle at that, picture suburban lawn gnomes, jockeys, junkies.

"Hi," I say.

Squid opens his eyes and groans.

"You fell asleep."

He sits up. "How long?"

"I don't have a watch," I say. "Not too long."

He looks at me as if he can't place me, then remembers, he says, "Katey," with surprise and opens his mouth like he's about to continue, then doesn't. He feels the blanket around his shoulder, realizes he's not wearing a shirt. "Shit," he says. He looks at me, and pulls it around himself. "What are you doing here?"

I say nothing and he asks, "Did you come here looking for me?"

"I was already here," I begin. "I was thinking. My sister used to come here. Back in the day."

"Your sister?" he asks.

"Reese," I say. "My older sister."

"Used to be a wild place. No one comes here anymore. He rubs the top of his head, waiting for me to agree. "I feel like shit. This wasn't," he says carefully, searching for the right words, "my usual stuff." He stands up slowly, knees popping, and moves into the drier brush. His back is to me and the blanket falls off his shoulders as he bends to pick something up. It's his shirt. "Want to get a drink?" he calls. "Let's get a drink. You and me." He pauses, then, "I have some money."

"Wait," I say. "I need to do something first."

I stand up and stamp my feet. My extremities are close to numb from the chill and sitting. I find a forked branch, twice my height, and hitch the swing rope by a knot. Pulling it into my hands, I toss it up into the highest boughs and face the maple; handholds hacked into the trunk's side, healed into beige keloidal scars, and my fingers fit into the smooth grooves. The climb takes a few minutes, and towards the top, the holds disappear, and it's a guessing game as to which branches will hold my weight. Some crack beneath me, but finally, I edge onto the right limb, untangle the swing, and hold on.

"You going to jump?" Squid yells.

"Yes," I call, not even realizing that was what I was here for. But as I say that, my resolve softens, and I lean out, the branch bowing under me, and look down into the pond. It's black and glassy, and I can't tell exactly where I should land, if I should go at all, and I study it some more, when I'm hit by a feeling much worse than I've felt, that I can remember, but anyway I release and go, my hands sore with cold and friction, slipping down, and this sensation lasting longer than the jump, than the stun of the water, than Squid enclosing me in the blanket at the bank, than the smell of wet wool and vomit, than wringing out my jacket, this sensation of falling lasting until I follow Squid, dripping wet, the half mile to the road, then two blocks to a bar.

The bar has no name, just an awning. No one stares at us when we walk in. I sit at a wobbly table, drape my wet coat over the back of a chair. He orders four scotches, and brings them over on a small tray, just like a waiter.

"That was a stupid thing to do," he says, but not displeased, laying two drinks in front of me. He says this down at my wet shirt.

"Thanks," I answer. "I'd never done that."

"Not me," he says, shaking his head like we were actually discussing the fate of a third with pity and scorn. "I only go there when it'd be too dangerous to be out, you know?" he asks. "When I need to," he starts, but doesn't finish, sadly looks at his drink. "I'm safe there. It's a safe place for me."

"Sure," I say. I try to sound encouraging.

"Not my usual stuff this time," he repeats. "So I was bad?"

"Weird," I answer. I sip at the scotch. It opens my nose like a menthol rub. He gulps his down quickly.

"It was like being in *Waiting for Godot*," I say.

"Was I Panzo?" He smiles and sucks on an ice cube.

"Pozzo," I correct. "Panza was in *Don Quijote*."

"Pancho," he says.

"No," I say. "You're thinking Pancho Villa."

"Yeah," he says. "I guess." He spits the ice back into the glass, then at once, we both blurt, "Fucking Mrs. Bellingham," and laugh.

Then it's over; he stabs at his drink with the stirrer. "You always liked that, Katey."

The jukebox plays country a measure too slow, and I barely touch my second scotch.

"Robinson Caruso," he says. "*Waiting for Godot*. I never understood that shit."

"Yes," I argue. "You did."

He grabs my drink and downs it, places it back upside down. "What the fuck you doing here, Katey?"

"You wanted me to help you," I say. It sounds stupid.

"How the fuck can you help me?" He laughs tightly. "What are you going to do for me?"

"What about you?" I ask.

"I'm dying," he says. "What are you doing?"

I wait for him to go on.

He holds up his hand. "What you want from me,

Katey?" He frowns at me. "Jesus. Two lives, Katey. Which one's the bullshit?"

I grab my jacket and stand up.

"That's it," he says. "Now you got the right idea. Get the fuck out of here."

I'm frozen to the spot. I look him over, try to memorize him. "You're not the only one." It's the only thing I can think of to say.

He picks up a glass and shakes it. He looks back at me, then looks down. "Hey, sorry," he says. "Maybe I was lucky you were there. Fucking lucky." He doesn't mean it, but his eyes have changed. He sees something, he thinks, something to take, but I back up.

"Lucky," he says again, then I hear my voice saying "Bye, Squid," but what I'm thinking is, What is luck anyway but being in the right place at the right time? Or the wrong one.

★

InkCredible is exactly where I remember, next to the beauty supply store on Main Street. I am not sure if that was where I meant to go.

Our mother used to tell us it was full of bad people, bikers. She was afraid; she held our hands.

This interested Reese very much. It just made me think of Dr. Rollins. Dr. Rollins wasn't a bad person; he was our dentist. His office a second floor storefront, the blinds open so he could keep an eye on his Kawasaki, parked out front. It was a beast of a thing, a Chinese dragon, all silver and locust green. He had a small tattoo on his wrist, but he tugged his sleeve over it. His hands were gentle stretching my mouth open, speckled pink and white like uncooked bacon, and his face, pinched the same pastel, his sad little ponytail held by a baggy rubber band, and his eyebrows: he always looked surprised or embarrassed to be scraping at my teeth.

Maybe I don't recognize danger. Like women on TV talk shows, in love with serial killers, standing by their rapist husbands. Maybe danger and uncertainty, maybe this is what I know.

The man with the motorcycle is no killer, no rapist, but what he offered me, what I took: you could just never be absolutely sure. I was never sure.

But this is what I know. I followed him. I thought he was dangerous, what I've been prepared for. But he isn't. He's something else.

The first time I'd been inside InkCredible was with Reese.

Little Neel didn't even let us get a word in. When you're eighteen, he said, crossing his arms. He didn't look bad either, muscles boldfaced and filled with air. He wasn't little by a long shot, and it made me think of nicknames.

For awhile, I tried giving Reese a nickname. I tried calling her Cup or Candy.

Cup, she snapped, sounds like a bra, and Candy, like I'm a whore.

When you're eighteen, Little Neel repeated.

Man, Reese whined, Maybe I won't ever see eighteen, and eighteen came and went and Reese never mentioned a tattoo again, although she dealt Neel a little heroin and some mushrooms, but not much. He used heroin only once in awhile, and Reese barely ever had mushrooms. She ran with a different crowd.

The second time was my own eighteenth birthday. I pushed through the door feeling lucky and sophisticated and dangerous, and I picked out the best flash I could afford. It was a nickel-sized calla lily, on the fatty part of my inner arm.

My friend Michael taught himself on baloney and chicken skin. He was beautiful, a toddler's face on a man's body, oversized pants. He'd fall asleep next to me fifteen minutes into Art History lecture, slavering a pool across his desk.

Michael didn't have a motorcycle. He drove a rattle-canned Plymouth Valiant and worked towards a sculpture degree. He didn't have a good baritone. He hadn't traveled much at all.

Finals week, we tabled our studying and he gave me a tattoo.

To watch over you, he said.

I liked that, a gargoyle on my lower back so I'd have to take off my shirt. His hands swabbing ink and blood from my skin 11:30 pm: snow under the streetlamps too bright to look at. High on adrenaline and lust, it burned like a fire.

Worse than my first, I said to him. Feels like I've been shot.

Michael stepped off the pedal and the needle stopped. You've never been shot, then? he asked in an action hero pose, motorized uh's rolling from the back of his throat like a machine gun, and we laughed. It was a stupid joke.

Never really held a gun, I answered.

We fired his .357 at midnight on the dot, the explosion a melody compounded with thousands of screams, student screams, a finals' week tradition at the university.

I held the gun out at the tree. Michael laughed at my wrists, weak under the gun. He stood behind me, his chest against my bare back, the tattoo sticky under the bandage. For that moment, he was mine. My finger on the trigger, his hands my hands and we pulled, breathing together; the burst of gas, a split second shine, then I slammed limply against his chest, trying to catch my breath while he held his.

We didn't speak. He ran back into the shop, slamming the bathroom door. I waited, gathered my shirt, wondering if he came in his pants. I never saw him again.

The inside of InkCredible is warm and bright, buzzing and silence from the back room. I settle on the couch and pretend to flip through tattoo magazines heaped on the table. Pond water beads off me, spreading sulfuric and dark across the carpet, and the magazine pages gum together between my fingers, so I toss them back and sink into the pillows.

Someone shakes me awake, a thin woman with a shaved head, glasses, and overalls. "Are you waiting?"

I nod and she backs up to let me stand.

"You're wet," she says.

I look down. It looks like someone opened a hydrant across the floor. "Sorry about that."

She holds up her hand. It's green and purple with violets, a bumblebee, an angel. "I didn't know it was raining." She holds out the same hand. "Natalie Pashelle."

I shake it, can't remember where I've heard that name, then I realize, the phone card. Then I know and I blurt out, "Someone stole your wallet."

This startles her. "You a psychic or something?" She looks puzzled, then suspicious. "How do you know?"

"Someone tried to sell me your phone card," I start, trailing off, and she stares at me and I get nervous, fiddle with a loose string on my cuff. "Today."

"Hope you didn't buy it. It's canceled now. They stole my whole wallet," Natalie says, turning away and shaking her head sadly. "The other day. There wasn't even anything worth anything, know what I mean?" She pauses. "At least not to anyone but me."

"Yeah," I say.

"Thanks anyway." She squints at me. "Is that all?"

"No," I answer, not moving. I feel ridiculous. "I came by for a tattoo. Actually."

She opens her mouth to say something, then changes her mind and waits for me to answer.

"I don't have an appointment," I go on, quietly, reverently, and this brightens her up, she trusts me a bit more and stretches her arms above her head.

"I can do that right now," she says. "Unless you want a whole sleeve."

I shake my head at that. "A little one," I say.

She walks briskly to the counter and places a clipboard on my lap. "Read and sign."

I do and hand it back to her.

"ID?"

I hand her my license. "OK . . . Katey," she reads, then smiles at me. "Las Vegas, huh? You lucky?"

"Sometimes."

"Well, let's go."

I follow her to the back room. Natalie grabs a thin brown robe off a hook, the kind they provide at fancy salons, and thrusts it at me. "Put this on," she says. "We can let your clothes dry some, yeah?"

I look gratefully at her and tug off my damp clothes. Natalie sits at a drafting table and watches me, tongue over her teeth.

"You're a bitty thing," she says. "Bet you fluff up when dry though." She's taller and thinner than I am, but I can see by the frustration on her face that she's never been graceful, never considered herself so; but right now, she seems beautiful to me. She laughs to herself, than turns back to the desk and feeds a pencil into a sharpener. "So, why you wet, anyway?"

"I jumped the swing," I answer.

"Jesus. I thought they took that down."

"No."

"You drunk?"

"No," I say. "Not really."

"You crazy?" She laughs at that. "So, what are you thinking of?"

"Right now?" I ask, then realize what she means, and say "Oh," but she stops me, "No, now," and laughs again, gently.

I tie the sash, and she faces me. "I'd like a cameo," I say. "Over my heart."

She thinks about this, chewing on the eraser, then says, "Like an old time brooch? The kind grandmas wear at their collars?"

I nod. "That's it."

"My grandma had one of those," she says.

And I describe it, the roundness, the transparent pink shell, the fine profile, the buff of warm cream; I can see it as clearly as when Reese pinned it onto me.

She begins to sketch and motions to me. I peek over her shoulders and watch her draw. "Like that?"

"Yes."

She holds the paper up. "Pretty unusual. What's it for?"

I think about that. "I want something," I say, "that nobody can steal."

*

I walk the grate back towards Shay's: a re-enforced steel drainage duct that runs behind Main Street and along the highway. It ends at the west gate of St. Stephen's Cemetery, and I follow the gravel path towards the center of the cemetery where it converges with the other paths, north, south, and east.

I thought I'd forgotten that, but when I step into the grass, I knew I meant to come here.

One time, Reese told me, I don't sleep. It's too much like death.

Is that what it's like? I asked.

She wasn't expecting that. She was quiet for awhile. I don't know, she finally answered. Maybe. I'll come and tell you. When I go, she went on, I'll come back and tell you.

We must have been in bed, because I buried my face in her neck. This is the way I remember it.

When are you going to go?

Soon, she said. Probably soon.

How do you know you're going to die? I asked.

Oh, she said. We're all going to die.

Take me, I said. When you go, take me with you.

Katey, she answered, or maybe: Katherine.

Then I said, I don't want to be here alone.

I loved her, maybe with madness. I thought that, without her, I'd be alone. But I said that to please her. I knew it was a lie. Lying is easy.

I have always been alone.

That last time, the last time I see her alive, she holds my head out the window and I watch the sunlight in pieces across the concrete, the elevated tracks grinding, sparking under a train.

I wanted her to break my neck. Do it, I thought. But I didn't say that. I said nothing. I wanted to mean it, to think and to believe it. I always wanted to mean it. Reese taught me close to everything, and regardless, I wanted to live. It wasn't just her hands at my throat, it wasn't fear. Always and again, I said nothing.

And that moment, I turn and see her face. In that moment, I looked at her, realized she was already gone.

★

Each grave in St. Stephen's seems the same as the others, each tooled name swimming in my vision without registering in my head, and I read the names quickly to myself, Montgomery, Murphy, Spiro, until I'm confused. Identical slices of marble shade small rises, resembling distended stomachs, for a mile in a perfect square. The grass is thicker and healthier than any I've ever seen, especially for October, each blade broad, sharp, and more blue than green. Compact trees line the paths towards the center, and it takes me a few minutes to walk through to the stone benches. I sit down, look out at the main north gate somehow foolish in its bent iron magnificence, gothically looming over the squat trees and tombstones, over the highway running past it.

This is a stupid idea, I think to myself. I should leave. Birds trill from a low tree, and I wish I had a cigarette or something. I'm discouraged, and I realize, listening to the birds, that I could be having some transcendent moment, that if I were a different person I could write a poem, think something beautiful and meaningful; I search for a metaphor, but my hands flap uselessly at my sides. If I were a different person, I could feel sad; I could've told them all already, but I'm not yet a different person, although each minute I feel it happening. I look across the cemetery, each a perfect white tablet, evenly spaced, geometrically placed, and what seemed confusing to me walking through now appears actually quite orderly, like perfect patchworked crops seen from an airplane. This calms me a bit; that death is not the equalizer for the deceased, but for the remaining. All of the dead, good or evil in life, find the same space, lying proudly, manicured, subsequent to another, each as worthy of grief as the next. Then I notice, down by the east fence, some smaller memorials set into a marble wall and I know that's what I'm looking for. He's got to be there.

I follow the path, then veer off, weaving around plots until I reach the last cremation memorial.

Donald Levitt Horvath, 1973-1995, Beloved Son

I was a good student. My options, my dreams. For instance, I loved Greek drama. There was something about it I understood, blood and revenge. When I was in high school, I wrote an essay on the *Oresteia*. I don't remember it all clearly and, silly as it seems, I think of that paper as I stand here. Orestes haunted in Athena's Temple by voices, the voices of the Furies, and he holds out the hands that killed his mother.

And while my life is not a Greek drama, maybe it is. This is the closest to a metaphor I can get. I had to kill my sister; I let her die. I need to tell you I'm the type of girl who spilled her own blood. I did this through silence—I could have saved her, I must have been able to save her, I would have saved her if I could, there was nothing to do, I was too late—maybe all, all of these are true.

Anyway, this essay was the best in the class. I read it to a state panel at an English teachers' conference held at a hotel on the interstate. I was, as the teachers said afterwards, full of promise. But right before I went on, Mrs. Bellingham, mistaking my silence for fear, told me to just be myself. I was prone to bruising or nosebleeds before exams, presentations.

Just say hello, she said. Picture them in their underwear, and now I cannot stop myself. I picture Don in a pair of boxer shorts in the parking lot that birthday, his frail legs and carved out chest, placing the Thinsulate hat on my head gently, his watery eyes hopeful. He leans against the car, and reaches out to touch me.

When it happened, his death, I didn't think much of it, or of him. His memorial was a Saturday; I hung back with Annika, breathing tequila out the sides of our mouths. His mother was beautiful with anguish and grief; it seemed the service was for her alone. The mourners circled around her, holding hands and bowing heads, and I remember watching, as if from a great distance. I felt uncomfortable and out of place, as if I'd arrived too late to be of help, or I'd forgotten my lines in a play.

Don's mother saw us eventually. She clutched us to her and cried, spotting fine white crusts of salt and mucus on our shoulders.

"Thank you," she said to us.

She held our cheeks and our hands, and we tried to be graceful. We patted her back and kissed her hairline up where it was dry. We lowered our eyes and pretended that was strength, sorrow.

"Donald was lucky to have such friends," she said. "So lucky."

And again, what is luck? I was there, I was in his class. I chose nothing, no effort, no enterprise. If he loved me, I didn't notice. I bowed my head and pretended that was sadness.

"And," she continued, "I never got to say goodbye."

I opened my mouth and something came out. It sounded like, "We never get to say goodbye."

His mother cried again at that, but gratefully. She pulled me to her. She held me for my humanity. But when she held me, I looked over her shoulder.

And now: I stand above Don's memorial. I think of him, I think of Reese. I could have saved her, I must have been able to save her, I would have saved her if I could, there was nothing to do, I was too late—maybe all, all of these are true. But if things are true, the most true thing is how I let her die for my own freedom.

I have always been alone.

Whatever you hurt, you keep forever.

SEVEN

Back at Shay's, my eyes take a minute to get adjusted; all I can see are shadows, and shadows can take on different shapes. Her apartment only draws the morning sun, and is already dusk black. I undershoot the stool and land hard the four feet from window sill to carpet. I pick myself up, then scuff across to avoid slamming my shins, and grope for the overhead light. I blink a few times at the brightness, then I notice Danny.

"You smell like shit," he says. He's sitting on the edge of the bed holding some yellow flowers in a tissue-paper spindle carefully between his hands, as if he weren't careful, it'd spill. He stares over me at the window.

"You scared me," I say. "How'd you get here?"

"Same way you did," he says. He doesn't turn from the window or meet my gaze.

I think about that. "I doubt that." I walk over and turn on the other light, in the kitchen, grabbing my pack on the way. "I'm going to change," I call, and stand behind the refrigerator where the view is obscured. I suddenly feel very shy, but the silence is more unnerving, and as I pull a dry shirt and pants from my pack, I call out again, "Are those chrysanthemums?"

"Yes," he says, suddenly standing at the kitchen door. I must look surprised to see him there; he says, "It's not like I haven't seen you, Katey," and I'm about to say, "This feels different," but don't. He looks at me completely without interest, still squeezing the bouquet, the tissue crumbling between his fingers. So instead I say nothing for a minute, hoping he'll say something, tugging on my jeans, a lighter falling from the pocket as I jump a little, urging them up my damp legs. Danny flinches at the clatter the lighter makes, blinks stupidly, and steps backwards.

"Want a vase for those?" I ask, buttoning my fly. I toss my dirty clothes into the sink and peel the bandage from my chest. The tattoo is bright and raised, glossy with cream and blood, and I turn to face Danny, but he's moved back to Shay's bed and sits in his original position. I rinse the tattoo with warm tap water and pat it with my shirt, then look in the cabinets. There's not a vase, so I fill a coffee mug with water, and see, behind the mugs, Shay's stash of cigarettes. Danny doesn't make a sound, so I pull one from the pack and light it off the gas burner.

"You smell like shit," he repeats. "Eggs or something."

"No," I say, exhaling. "Now I smell like smoke."

"These," he says, holding up the flowers, "are for your sister." He looks sadly at my face. "I'm sorry."

He stares at me for what must be a few seconds, at most, but feels like five full minutes, then looks away, his eyes catching color like oil or fish scales. He looks like he's about to cry, and I feel a vein pulse in my neck. He knows, I think in a panic, everybody knows. I can't imagine my expression, fear and relief maybe, shock, and I look back at him, tears rolling down his cheeks fully now, everything in slow motion, as if I were witnessing a terrible accident from a full second before it happens and am powerless over its occurrence.

"I don't want to hurt you, Katey," he finally chokes out, "but I never meant to hurt Shay either." He holds the flowers up to his face and breathes them in, and I suddenly want to laugh, it's hilarious, but I feel terrible too, and if I started, I'd be unable to stop. I wait for some kind of punchline. "We made a mistake."

"They're for Shay?" I ask. "The chrysanthemums?"

Danny wipes his eyes with a sleeve. "They're her favorites, you know. Chrysanthemums."

"No," I answer, ashing into the mug. "I didn't know that."

"I'm in love with her."

"Hmmm," I say, unsure what else there is.

"And I fucked up.You're her sister."

"Yes," I say. "I sure am." I look at Danny; he holds his head in his hands. It's all very dramatic. I finish the cigarette and drop it into the cup.

"You're so different than she is." Danny stares at me again, silently. "I guess," he finally says, "I thought you'd be the closest I'd get to her." He half hiccups. "There's no good answer."

"Well," I start, then stop, and look at the clock. It's

3:30. "This isn't going to look good then either. She's coming home soon."

He places the flowers across his lap carefully, pulls off his baseball hat and runs his fingers through his hair. He waits for me to go on.

"Leave the flowers with me. I'll explain everything."

Danny looks at his lap. I motion towards the bouquet and hold out an arm.

"Let me talk to her, Danny." I pat his shoulder. "It'll work out."

His face looks hopeful. "You think so?"

"Sure," I say, and as I do, I almost believe it. Danny places the flowers into my arms nervously. I have left him no choice. In the exact center of his eyes I can see my own face looking out, warped and huge. "You're in love with my sister."

"Yes."

The tension is ridiculous. I can't take it. So, I sigh deeply, comically, to try and lighten the mood, play my hands on hips, turn and stomp across the room. "I'm always the last to know these things."

Danny watches me move towards the kitchen with the flowers. I force a smile at him one more time, but as I walk, I slow, moving like an old woman across the floor. Arthritic and graceless, the door seems yards away, and again, before me is a vision: ruined, fragile, and bald, toothless, nothing more than a dry tassel of bones.

"I'm always the last to know."

"Or the first," I hear Danny call slowly after me, "depending on how you look at it."

And I can see the woman I'll become in this instant, and I ache for her. I move in this body, in this becoming, and I'm not afraid. My life behind me, stretched out like a museum rope, marked by death, by failures, by international catastrophes, by the length of my nails. But too much separates us, these two me's, time and responsibility, and then the vision is gone again.

Too much separates us, and I feel powerless and weak: the insomniac waiting for sleep, the waiting itself keeping me awake.

I'm abandoned back into the present, I reach the door and spin back to face Danny, but he's already disappeared out through the window, and it's too late.

Hello, I hear.

It's his voice.

You've reached Katey and M. Not here, so, and then the beep, and I hang up, dial again, Hello, he says, You've reached, and it's his voice, rinsed and serious, Katey and M, so, and a longer beep.

I open my mouth, then shut it. I wonder if he misses me, what he's doing right this moment.

Now that I'm here, I remember my life like a story I've been told. Sitting in classes, taking notes: how did I decide what was important? The late desert sunset. Boiling spaghetti, first letting the strands soften so as not to break them before they sink below the water. I'm aware of how delicate, and even the tender snapping makes me wince. I miss something.

The answering machine cuts me off. I wonder what I'd say if I had the courage.

I can't decide if I'm disappointed or relieved that he's not answering. I can't decide if I'm not disappointed, why I'm so sad.

I hit the receiver down, hold it with a finger, then release; I dial Bill's direct line from memory, and it rings. A woman picks up, a wrong number, the wavery voice of the expectant and the infirm, and I realize I want to cry, and for the first time I do, tears like an idiot, and the woman says "Hello? Hello?" over and over, and I want to say something, say, Please don't hang up, please, this woman has no investment, in me, no interest, and I could say, Hello, don't hang up, my sister's dead, and I'm all alone, the man I love doesn't love me, not that I think, I haven't told anyone anything, my mouth won't work, but my mouth won't work now either, and I cry into the receiver until the woman goes, "Melanie? Is that you?"

I want to say "No," tell her who I am, who I am really, that maybe I wanted to protect my parents, my little sister, but I've been so bad, I haven't done the right thing. My parents, and Shay, the flowers already brown at the petals, if I thought of her, and maybe I wanted to protect all of them from Reese, but maybe then also, truly, at the end I'm as guilty, truly, maybe I wanted her, or I wanted everything all to myself.

The woman says, "Melanie," again, and I could say all this, but don't, what would that say about me? "Yes," I almost say, "Yes," and then the woman says, "Melanie, I can hear you crying," and I almost say, "Yes, it's me," because for a few seconds, I wish it was so, whoever and wherever Melanie is, I want it to be so.

I think back to M, that day. I laughed like a child to find he was right: the drinking glass we left full of water on the nightstand, now empty, dry, and frosted with minerals.

You see? he asked. It's true. Gone within an hour. He looked at his watch. Or two.

Where is it? I kidded him then.

He pointed up. The sky, he said. The sky.

★

The woman says "Hello?" one last time, then hangs up, and I fold, listening to the tone until it fades into, Your call cannot be completed, and I think to myself, Neither can I.

"Precinct fifteen, McDonnell speaking," and I say, "Bill Keene, please. Katherine Bruscke." I hold to Patsy Cline's "Walking After Midnight," *searching for you*, and then the click of a transfer.

"Bill Keene."

Typing in the background, something else that sounds like a buzzsaw, and I say, "Hi, Bill." I try to sound cheerful.

"Katherine. We have to talk." I realize this means, I have to talk at you, so I let him, and he says some things, then "The autopsy's in. I have a complete *corpus delicti*. Made any decisions?"

"Decisions?" I repeat.

"Funereal," he says. He pauses. "Have you even told your family?"

"You didn't tell me the whole story," Bill says to me.

"I would have had to start a long time ago."

★

I think of photos never taken. Reese resting her hand lightly on my arm, a bland loving smile, but her nails hooking, tearing into the underside of my wrist.

This could be anytime, this particular snapshot.

In reality, I was too much the little sister; always hanging back, listening, not a perfect reflection, and for this, I must be punished. I helped her pack her clothes in garbage bags like a child cutting a switch for their own beating. I knew what this meant. These photos never taken became a legacy. We could both be erased, she thought, with no one to avenge us.

★

This is what Bill tells me: October 15, 12 to 1 pm, Reese settles on the couch. It is a velour and imitation leather loveseat.

Football is on every channel. There is no VCR.

The house is not hers; it belongs to some guy serving a three year sentence for battery, two counts, and possession of narcotics with intent to distribute. The house is a old one-story cracker-box on the east side of downtown, one main room, a captain's kitchen, and a bathroom. There is a Murphy bed, pulled down. The doors are locked but the windows facing the street are wide open. It is still seasonable, sixty degrees, negligible humidity.

First, Reese smokes a rock of crack. There isn't much, but it's all there is. She'd already searched through the drawers. She drinks a can of sweetened condensed milk to take the edge off.

Then it's blank until sometime after 1:45, sometime before two. It's uncertain whether Reese heard them enter, even imagined three shots from a snub-nosed Smith and Wesson.38. She never even got up. Didn't even try.

This is what he tells me: two penetrating shots. The fatal wound, the third, of the perforating type to the anterior chest wall, entrance ten millimeters, four centimeters of gunpowder tattooing, and no soot. She was shot from less than two feet away.

I never got past her hands. Those hands rapping at my bedroom door: Katey, she whispers, let me in.

Katey. I can't sleep.

Save me, Katey. Save me.

I pull my pillow over my head; I cannot hear her stay or go. When I open my eyes, it will be morning.

I have no other choice. I cover my ears.

Whatever you hurt, you keep forever.

*

Bill taps the phone with his nails. He waits for my response. "Twenty four hours, Katherine."

"Thank you," I say, barely above a whisper. "That's all I need."

"You need to tell your parents." He sighs loudly. "This is just between us, civilian to civilian. Friend to friend."

"Are we friends?"

"That's not the point."

"I would have done it."

"But you didn't."

"No," I say.

"This is just irregular. Did you think you could fool me?"

"I understand."

"You lied to me."

"I was afraid."

"You're lying to me again."

"No."

"You didn't tell me you had family."

"Did you ask?"

"Now," he answers. "That isn't the point either."

I hold the phone and wait.

Bill sighs. "Irregular," he repeats. "Not procedural. Did you think I wouldn't find out?"

"I'm sorry," I say.

"Why, Katherine? Between us."

"It's my fault."

"This is beyond martyrdom."

"I don't know much about God."

"What do you need to know?"

"Do you believe in God, detective?"

"Sometimes. A little."

"What is God?"

He pauses, seems to think about that. "God is love, Katherine. Love." He recites this ironically, without much conviction.

"Who will love me now, detective?"

"You tell them, or I will." He's losing patience with me.

"The opportunity hasn't shown itself," I say. It sounds like TV. "The time has to be right."

"Katherine. There is no right time."

"Tonight," I say. "I'll tell them tonight."

"Or else, I send an officer, Katherine," he says stiffly, "in twenty four hours."

★

The front door catches me off guard. I hadn't considered there to be a front door at all, even though there is one. I'd been watching for Shay out the window, but she opens the door and pulls it across the thick carpeting in the corridor. From what I can see, the hall is long and poorly lit, and wafting with a pissy detergent odor. Shay pulls the door closed again; she seems surprised to see me there, sitting on her bed cross-legged, and she takes me in for a second, as if trying to remember where we know each other from. I wonder what it is she sees, but then she's inside and drops her bag.

"Long day," she says. "You?"

"OK," I answer.

She nods slowly, as if just understanding, and throws her coat over the back of a chair, gets herself a beer. "You cleaned up," she says simply, then takes a long drink. She walks over and sits next to me. "Thank you."

I nod, and she offers me the bottle. I drink then pass it back to her. She waves it away and reaches under her shirt, unclasping her bra. She pulls it out an armhole, and lets it drop to the floor. "I have to shower," she says. "I did deliveries today. I feel dirty." She unbuttons her shirt on her way to the bathroom, and leaves the door open a crack. A thin shelf of steam filters out the door. I lie back on the bed.

"What did you do today?" she calls.

"Not much," I say. "Rested."

"Good."

She showers, the apartment filling with the tarry smell of lavender. The water shuts off, and Shay bends over by the mirror in her plaid robe, flipping her clumpy wet hair forward. She chops at it with a comb. "You look nice in my shirt," she says.

"Thanks," I answer. "I should borrow from you more often."

Shay moves to her closet. "Where are my sweaters?" she asks.

"I folded them."

She pushes wet hair from her face. "Why?"

I sit up and drop my legs over the side of the bed. "Come here," I say. "Bring the comb."

She sits on the floor between my legs, and I divide

hanks of her hair, laying the sections across her head and face. Then I begin to pull them one by one away from her head at forty-five degree angles and comb through. "I remember when you had little bowl cuts."

Shay laughs through her hair. "Mom," she says.

"Want a braid?"

She nods.

"You have to sit still." I press my palms flat against her temples and squeeze. She wriggles out of my hands and scoots forward. "Wait. I have some rubber bands in the kitchen." She stands up. "And there's Vaseline by you." She walks back into the kitchen and this time I hear her say "Oooooh," rushing back in holding the mug of chrysanthemums. I'd forgotten about them, and she's beaming at me, eyes all pupils, and says, "These are for me?" and I'm about to say "Yes, from Danny," and I get out the "Yes," and she places them on the desk and rushes over to hug me.

"They're beautiful," she says, the words falling into one another. "I wanted you to just rest."

"But," I say weakly, then finish, "they're your favorites."

Shay kisses my cheek, then moves back and smells them, holding back her wet hair. Then she looks up happily, pulls them from the cup and shakes the excess water off the stems.

I watch her bury her face in the petals and wonder if she'd always been this easy to please.

A bottle breaks in the next apartment, and another, thrown against the common wall between Shay and, I realize, Danny's. The walls are thin. Was he listening?

Shay turns to the noise and I can't see her expression, but her fragile shoulders rise and fall slightly, and she waits; as the third bottle breaks she storms over to the wall, holding the chrysanthemums above her head, and kicks. "Asshole," she says, under her breath. "Fucking, fucking asshole." She attacks again, kicking hard, and it silences Danny, it silences me, her rage. A headache like a cap on top of my head beats and pulls, and then she turns, white and sweaty, her eyes strange.

"Shay," I say. I want to end the moment. She smoothes her hair back from her face and listens. "You forgot the rubber bands, Shay."

She gets them, hands them to me, and settles back onto the floor between my knees. I take another drink of the beer and pass it down to her, positioning her head away from the wall. I resume my combing, relieved I have a few rubber bands between my teeth. I don't know what else to say.

We sit in silence, Shay bows and turns her head under my hands, and I work a wide, straight, achingly white part, attempting to lure the sections into a smooth braid.

Her hair is thick and coarse, just like mine, just like Reese's, and as if reading my mind Shay sighs, then. "You know," she says, "I used be jealous of you. Reese always braided your hair."

I blink a few times, the small work making me cross-eyed. "Mmmm."

"She paid attention to you," she says.

I blink a few more times. All I have is what I can see.

A few bands fall from my mouth, bounce across the bed.

"Shay," I say. "You've got the family hair. Dry like plastic."

"I condition it."

"Pomade or something," I answer. "You need something oily. But not Vaseline."

"Can we get some tomorrow?" she asks. "Will you help me pick out some?"

I don't answer, and then she asks, "Will you be here still tomorrow?"

"Shay," I say, and open my mouth, but she sighs deeply out her nose and hushes me, whispering back, "I know," and then again, "I know, I know," and then quiet. She rests her head on her knees for a moment, and I hold up my hands, spread my fingers, as if drying nailpolish. She doesn't really know, but it's all right. We are a still-life, the two of us, sisters.

Silence settles over us, and I work on finishing her braid.

Shay stands up and admires herself in the mirror. "Mom was useless with hair."

"Yeah. Mom."

She blows a kiss at herself, then looks at me like she didn't mean it. "You left me alone with her all this time. Why?"

"Come here," I say. "It's not done."

Out the window, night has fallen, the moon slapped yellow, flat against black, pine trees peeling away from the sky like paint, the time of night where everything outside becomes its own shadow, and shadows, shadows can be anything.

I hook the rubber band around the hank, and tuck in the loose hairs. Shay reaches up and grabs my hands, not moving her head, and pulls them down to touch her face. "It's—" she starts. "It's time to go."

EIGHT

The only remarkable feature of our parents' neighborhood is the Post Office. It is built like the Temple of Athena. Their house is a '50s split level, two-story built late for this town. It is a rental, a fetish of overplanning and neglect: the paint peeling in silky husks, a leftover basketball hoop from prior tenants, tarnished green and drooping like a noose. New lawn furniture, a whitewashed wicker chair and glass table stand next to the threadbare tire swing. Hearty geraniums and skeletal tomato plants crowd the sun-faded tiles of the walkway, cracking like the tough skin of feet.

Growing up there required balance and endurance and a photographic recall of topography, but still midnights of stubbed toes, each of us victim to our mother's whims, her pathologies: a new coffee table, ottoman, freestanding leopard lamp.

This was never a house for children, not children, as the saying goes, decent children—how the three of us didn't have major accidents, something disfiguring, I don't know—toddling around half-finished highballs of scotch, frozen pizza dinners, scissors and open prescription bottles.

Then I think it's never too late for an accident. I push Reese from my mind.

Shay looks at me as if I'd said something aloud, the beaded curtain clacking behind us. She moves into the front room, bangs her knee against a life-sized porcelain Doberman pinscher, and closes her eyes in pain. "That's new," she hisses.

"Jesus," I whisper at her. "I'd almost forgotten."

She swallows, regains her composure. "Mom, Dad," she calls. "We're here."

But our mother's presence, her smell preceding her into the hallway, cotton-candied gaudy perfume, cocoa butter, and bleach, and then she floats towards us, seeming larger than the room, arms held slightly above her head wearing a bat-sleeved caftan, the hem catching on the carpet.

Our mother stops at the statue, caressing across the lacquered fur, and taps her fingers on the dog's head. One of her red acrylic nails is missing, and the cuticle is shriveled and pink. "Who got hurt?" she asks. "You or him?"

Shay points at herself. Our mother's hands flutter purposelessly, like nervous birds, then she touches one delicately to her chest. "Do you like? He's Italian."

"He doesn't look Italian," I say.

She turns toward me. "Let me look at you." She lets her hands come to rest on my shoulders. "Oh," she says. "You're lovely."

"Mom," I answer.

She crosses her arms like a corpse and moves into my chest for a hug; I awkwardly hold her elbows. She sighs, steps back, and at that moment slaps me directly across the face. It is for not calling, and we all know this. Shay shifts her weight foot to foot. Scald raises to my cheeks, and our mother watches me, testing me: waiting for me to reach up, hold my hands to the sting in defense, pinch out tears. Instead, I smile carefully, widen my eyes, suck in my stomach; I try to look like something she could love. I can't interpret her expression, mouth gathered, pink lipstick striping creases into her wrinkles, and my mind wanders in that moment. I realize what a beautiful woman our mother was, how you can still see in her eyes, the way she holds her hand fisted at her hip, how she looked in photographs, that men fought over her, and looking at me she sees herself at my age, or that she knows I've been here for two days. She stares back at me; I don't know what she reads from my expression. She turns away first.

"My darling," she says, eyes half closed, reaching out fully to me. "I missed you."

⋆

Shay and I follow our mother into the living room, and sit on the edge of the white linen couch. I rub at a purple stain on the arm, then turn, cover it with my back. Our mother watches me.

"You did that," she sighs. "Didn't you?"

"Grape juice," I answer, weakly.

Shay smacks her thighs, then hangs an arm across the couch back, over our mother. "Where's Dad?" she asks, brightly.

As if on cue, a door opens, releasing cheers throughout the house, then it stills, the sound waves absorbed by all the stuff crammed into every crevice. It's our father, I know, watching television, but our mother blinks softly, distractedly, patting Shay's arm, then stands, brushes the cushions and replaces the throw pillow so her place at the couch looks untouched.

"Your father is in the bathroom," she says, as if this was a joke or game of his, and rolls her eyes to signal that she's tired of it and to just play along. She moves towards the hall. "Bill," she yells. "Did you use the spray?"

He doesn't answer. "Bill," she yells again. "Come in here."

One heavy footstep and a drag, our father pulls his left leg behind him. "What?" This is from the hallway, to our mother. He stands, one hand pushing off the telephone table for support. "What are you talking, Tina? The spray?"

"The potpourri spray. You stink it up, Bill."

"Stink what?" He smoothes his bald spot. "Looks like Broncos going to make it to the Superbowl this year."

Our mother rolls her eyes. "The spray," she repeats, then exasperated, "Forget it. Just say hello to your daughters."

He holds his other hand up, to shade his eyes, as if he were looking directly into the sun. "Is that our Katey?"

I stand up. "Hi, Daddy."

He moves slowly into the room, grinning widely, head bobbing in something like a palsy. "Well," he says to me. "You're just too pretty now to look at straight on."

Every week for two years, our mother placed five dollars on lay-away for the dining room chandelier. I was sixteen when I helped her hang it, frosted glass sprays of art deco style flowers inlaid lilac and bordello maroon. Tonight, the light from it falls pink across the pot roast and peas making them appear artificial, fleecy with dust. We each stand behind our respective chairs around the table and stare at the food.

"This looks delicious," I say. "I'm ravenous."

Our mother looks at me suspiciously. "Your sister didn't feed you?"

Shay opens her mouth and closes it, like a fish. "Katey's been sick."

"Sick?" Our mother holds her stomach.

"No," I say.

"How sick?"

"Excuse me," Shay interrupts. "I'm going to wash up."

Our mother watches her go.

"Who's sick?" our father asks.

"No," I say, holding up my hands. "I'm fine."

Our mother absently picks up an empty glass from the table. "That's the good news then."

"The good news?" Our father looks confused. "What's the bad news?"

"Please, Bill. Bite your tongue." She looks around,

then leans delicately against the back of a chair. "Oh," she says. "Sciatica."

He shakes his head. "After dinner. If I have to hear bad news, not until after dinner."

"The good news is—" I say, interrupting, then pausing, not sure of what I'm going to say. "I'm going back to school."

Neither of our parents says anything at first, then our mother moves towards me and kisses the back of my head. She speaks into my hair. "You smell like smoke."

"That's all you have to say?"

"Well," she says. "That's wonderful, dear." She grimaces, clutches at her back. "We're proud of you, aren't we, Bill?"

"Tina," our father answers. "Sit down then, if it hurts."

"No, no." She hands me the empty glass. "What do you want to drink? Soda?"

"Fine," I answer. "That's fine."

"We don't have any soda. Not since you kids left."

Shay stands in the doorway. Our mother motions to her. "Shay, dear, go next door and ask the nice rabbi for a Coca-Cola. Tell him it's for me."

"Never mind. I'll have juice."

"No, no," our mother says. She shakes her head. "You want soda, we'll get a soda."

Shay glares at me, accusingly. "Katey's got legs if she wants a Coke."

"Mom," I say. "I'll get it."

This pleases her. "The rabbi moved next door, the yellow house, you know it."

I nod.

"Six kids," she goes on. "He must have a Coca-Cola. Tell him it's for me."

My feet sink in the mud and weeds beneath the dining room window. The light from the chandelier radiates out a cloudy light, as if it were raining inside our parents' house. I wait for a minute to hear if they say anything about me. Only late season crickets, nothing more.

The yard seems smaller, the yellow house closer than I remember, than summer afternoons playing Spud with Reese, the object of which seemed to peg me with a saggy red kickball.

The yellow house used to be the Garcías', then the McPhersons', and then I don't know. We never were friendly with neighbors, never played with the kids next door, so this is a change; but then I think, maybe not. Our mother didn't tell me the rabbi's name.

I walk up the lawn, firm under my sneakers. The blue of a television gleams from the front of the rabbi's house, ghostly and cold, like an illuminated aquarium. The porch is completely dark, and I try to adjust my eyes to see the steps when I notice a flicker brighten, then disappear.

"Hey," I call. No one answers and I walk forward, straight into a hand. It clamps over my mouth and pulls me back towards our parents' lawn. I think briefly about struggling, screaming, but the hand is curiously gentle, and I give myself over.

"Shhhh," someone whispers. "Be quiet. Not going to hurt you."

The hand drags me towards the square of dim dining room light. It's a boy, maybe sixteen, skinny and tall, glasses, in pajama pants. A cigarette hangs from the corner of his mouth and waves close to my cheek. "My father," he whispers. "He'd kill me." He waits to see if I understand.

I have a crazy thought, to stay out here, with him, his palm moist and smelling like a scab, but I nod and he releases me. "Hi," I say.

"Hi." In the light, his face shimmers like he's wearing makeup. He stares at my breasts and points at the house. "You live here?"

"Not anymore." I cross my arms. "My parents do."

The boy looks embarrassed, tears at the dead grass with his feet. "I'm Peter."

"Peter," I say. "You got any sodas?"

He shakes his head.

I point at his mouth. "You got another one of those?"

He hands me his. It's only half finished. "Have it." He looks over at his house. "I gotta go," he says, and moves out into the dark, disappearing like a ghost.

*

Back inside, the air hangs thick with meat. The food stands untouched across the table, like stage props. I follow murmurs into the living room, where my mother stands over Shay who empties her backpack.

"You're a good girl, darling," she says, as Shay hands her a bottle.

"This is syrup form, mother," Shay says. "I couldn't get the tablets." She holds the bottle to the light, and pulls a dosage cup from the neck. "You want no more than 100 milligrams." She waves the cup close to our mother's face. "No more than a finger. Do you see?"

"Oh yes," she says, and closes her eyes. "I see."

"Mother." Shay shakes her shoulders. "More than a finger, and I get in trouble." She shakes her again. "You hear?"

"Yes, I hear."

"They notice the tablets missing, but not the suspensions. Be careful to only take this much."

Our mother opens her eyes and takes the bottle, placing it on a side table. She seems to survey Shay's alarm, her insistence, and stretches an arm around Shay's shoulders, pulling her to her own neck.

Our little sister is stealing drugs.

No one sees me standing there for a minute, Shay nuzzling into our mother's neck, and I slowly back out of the room; they rock this way, as if in a dream, as if Shay had awakened from a long, bad dream, our mother's voice gentle, she says, "Now what did you get me for sleeping?"

I withdraw this way into the kitchen, backing up, the scene closing with the swinging door, and I bump into my father. He leans against the counter and shakes a glass at me, ice clicking. "Taste of scotch, Katey bear?"

"No," I say. "No thanks, Dad."

"Mmm. It's time to eat, I think." He drains his glass,

and spills the ice into the sink. "Get yourself a soda?" He watches the door as if he could see through it.

"They were out. I met the neighbor boy though."

"Yeah?" Our father stands behind me, presses his hand on my shoulder. "We knew it, you going to get your degree," he says. "We're all real proud of you."

I place my hand on his, one nail stamped deeply with calcium deposits, and lean back into his belly. "Thanks, Dad."

"Real proud of all you girls. You all found your own way." I feel us start to fall, but it is just our father leaning, taking weight off his leg. "It's bothering me," he says.

"What happened?" I ask. "Your leg?"

He smiles at me. "Time, Katey bear. Just time."

"Are you taking something for it?"

"No. Your mother seems to, though."

I cry out at that, almost without realizing. He drapes his arm around my neck, and my sobs are dry and soundless, bouncing against his stomach. "There, there," he says, "there, there, Katey. It's going to be OK, there."

His comfort seems to come from miles away. When I cry, it sounds like I am gasping for air.

"There are things you should've never seen," he says. "I'm sorry you did."

And what he actually means doesn't matter for now. In my mind I'm huge, I feel huge, looking down into the world, dollhouse-sized. Danny flat on his back in bed, counting and re-counting the lines in the ceiling, Annika eating off a paper towel, and Squid, asleep in a library restroom, and M, sweet M tinkering with a motor, or calling the answering machine from work, saying my name over and over again, Katey, Katey, Katey, until the tape runs out, the clouds close, fasten and lock; my father holding me, saying, "There, it's OK," and I want to know where, ask out loud, Where, my father holding me in a *heimlich* hug as if to push my words from my mouth, caught in the back of my throat, like medicine.

Shay sings along to *The Sound of Music*, loudly, and our father laughs, through the commercials. We can hear them across the apartment, sitting back on the couch, our mother holding a wet towel to her head.

"You used to love musicals," she says to me. "Remember?"

I fiddle with the coffee cup on my knee, running my finger damply along the rim like a monk playing prayer bells. "But I never sang."

"You used to sing. You had that song. What was that song?"

"What song?"

"You know which one, darling."

"No," I say. "I don't."

"The song you used to always sing." Our mother sighs, gives up, places the towel on her lap, and turns towards me. "You don't look good, darling." She lets her head fall back onto the back of the couch. "You need a shower. Fresh clothes."

"I thought you said I look lovely."

"Oh," she says. "It's lovely to see you."

"I'm not feeling that good."

"You are sick then?"

"No," I say, searching for the right word. "Inside."

"You ate too much?"

"No," I say, standing up.

"You can cry to your father?"

"I wasn't crying."

"I heard you crying."

Somewhere, a car alarm honks. It is loud, and our mother covers her ears. I place the cup down and move aimlessly around the room, picking things up and placing them a millimeter off from their places, marked by dust rings. This annoys her. She uncovers her ears and watches me like a painting.

"I'm thinking," I say.

I pick up a framed photo of Reese from a side table. It's not one that I've ever seen. Reese is robed and looking into the sky, her hands about to clap or to pray; it's difficult to tell which. I hold the frame up and wave it at our mother. "When's this?"

"You don't remember that?" she asks. "Reesy's graduation."

"Where's her mortarboard?"

"In the air," our mother answers, slurring, as if talking from sleep. "High up in the air."

I move back next to her on the couch, and she leans in towards me. "Where am I?" I ask. I mean in the picture, but our mother doesn't understand. The question rouses her. She opens her eyes. "Why darling," she answers. "You're right here."

"My little sad, brave one," she says. "Don't be sad." She tries to be a mother, and I let her. She feels for my knee, and I look at her hands, the back, veins laid across like piping. "You never let me help you," she says.

"It's like a bad dream," I say, quietly. Our father hoots from the other room.

"You always had those," our mother says. "I know this. Even though there weren't many nights you ran to me."

"What could you have done?"

"Exactly, my darling. Life goes forward. It's already too late."

I lean closer into our mother, and we topple sideways. She will not support the weight, exaggerates a wince, but I pretend not to notice. My heart beats, and we sit there. She eventually props a pillow under her back, and strokes my hands for awhile. She then begins to talk, her voice so insubstantial I fall in and out hearing the words, just the sounds. I feel as if I am dreaming, then I hear her say " . . . there's other boys, Katherine," she says. "You mustn't let him destroy you. There are always other men."

Like Shay, she also thinks I've broken with M, but I haven't the energy to correct her.

"My three girls. Reese always fighting like an animal to escape. Shay fighting herself. But you," she says. "You're always fighting spirits. The invisible. Voices."

Our mother runs her hands up my arms, as if to warm or wake me. Her nails scrape against my skin, leaving white trails of dead skin. She licks a finger and rubs at one. "This is the way you look, then I understand," she says. "You don't look so hot."

"Thank you," I answer. "Thanks a lot."

"Men," she says. "They like a pretty thing."

I don't answer her.

"Well," she says. "What did your father say about it? He said something better?"

"He didn't say anything."

"Of course not. What does he know about love?" She lays back with the towel and pats at her face. "Things disappear, people leave. And you don't look good, darling."

"But . . ."

"No buts. You have to care about the way you look for someone to care about you."

"It's Shay's shirt," I say.

She looks at me, as if over a pair of glasses. "Where are your clothes?"

"Dirty."

"You keep your clothes dirty? No wonder then."

"Mom," I say. "It's not that."

"OK," she answers, waving in the air. "You're right and I don't know anything."

"It's not that. It's not just that."

"My darling." Her voice is clear, weighted. She looks at me as if she can see me. "Nothing is ever just that."

"It's . . ." I say, then stop, our mother interrupting me.

"Go upstairs," she says. "At least put some cream on these elbows."

★

The upstairs bathroom holds all the same smells: hairspray, orange children's aspirin cut into the grout, combining to smell curiously like root beer. Even the towels are the same, polished bald with age so water runs off them into the yarn mat. Our mother's added a ceramic elephant, that when you pull the trunk, soap trickles out. It looks like something a child would like, the whole bathroom standing ready, footstool pushed under the sink and all. I pull my old toothbrush from the holder, rub it under the stream of sink water to wash the dust out, deep in its bristles. The dust peels off in rolls and clings to the drain, trembling linty caterpillars.

I remember reading that dust itself is sixty percent sloughed skin, twenty percent hair. This is what we leave behind. I pick out the dust and press it into a small cake, and lay it carefully on the sink. I wonder if any of it is Reese's.

This bathroom takes me to another time, wiggling a loose canine over this same basin, spitting blood like a prizefighter. A tin frozen in its own rust to the toilet tank filled with peel-off nailpolish, roll-on lipgloss, tiny seashell soaps.

Nights, watching Reese fix for a date, curlers, a face mask. I'd sit on the edge of the tub, and when she wasn't angry, when she was kind, she'd do the same to me.

Pay attention, little Katey, she'd joke. This is how you live a life.

I run the shower and bend over, letting the water hit my back, then begin to wash myself with a sense of purpose, preparation. I rub the little soaps over my body, pull a razor from a plastic basket.

I wash myself as if this were the last day of my life, and wonder what Reese did, that final day, morning. I wonder if she conditioned her hair, shaved her legs to her thighs, or if she stopped at the knees.

I switch off the water, reach for a towel, and balance the dust in my hands; I open the window inside the shower stall, the steam swelling thick and white out into the cool air. I stand at the window and hold my head out, looking around, I realize, like a fire, like I'm waiting for someone to save me, a damsel in distress.

I hold out my hands as if I too were about to clap or pray, let the dust roll from my palm. I watch it float, carried by a single blast of wind. It catches in the fleeting shine, headlights, cars passing by.

The bathroom cools, the swell of vapor from the shower tethered to the window frame by its own stream, its ceaselessness against the cold air; the house silent below me. The lights over the post office reflect against the marble, down the streets, luminous, dissolving dingy to the concrete. My skin crumpled like fabric from the shower, I lean out, hear the sound of a truck, watch the cars cruise by. One in particular pulls up, passes our parents' house, then reverses, backing up and into the driveway.

The motor cuts and the passenger side opens first, a body stepping into the headlights. They look up at the house as if surveying tornado damage and shake their head. The inside map lights glimmer weakly, and I can see the driver's silhouette apply lipstick, then they join the first, looking up at the house, and move towards the front door.

This is Annika's Beemer. I know this by the shape of the headlights. Some nights she'd drive, and I'd wait for her on the porch steps, the round headlights sharp yellow through the night, one like a lazy eye, roving off the side.

I throw on a bathrobe, the armholes sewn too far into the back, and run.

That first fire took everything away, it seems, and even though the smoke here is thin and white, perfumed, I can hear Shay saying, You can only save yourself. So I tie the sash and run, run downstairs as fast as I can, running forward, this time for sure as if I were about to save myself.

⋆

Our mother hasn't moved. She watches the door as the bell rings again.

M holds out a paper bag, Annika behind him, when I open the door. The hallway light hits their eyes and they squint at me.

"You," M says hoarsely. "You took the last suitcase."

"I left you the air conditioner," I say.

He tilts his head, as if to unclog his ears. "Is this how you say hello?"

"There's two under the bed," I say. "Suitcases."

He hasn't shaved, and stubble masks his face, clear as fishing line. "Can we," he says, and motions to Annika, who steps forward and smiles, "come in?"

"Oh god," I say. "Of course." I step back to let them in, and M waits, letting Annika through first.

She leans into me, kisses the air. "He called me," she whispers. "He didn't know what to do. So he called me."

I let her pass. M drops the bag in the doorway, and grabs me.

"Hello," he says. "Hi."

Our mother moves across the floor seemingly without legs, a landing pontoon, then holds Annika's shoulders. "Darling Annika," she says. "How lovely for you to come."

Annika squeezes her hands. "Mrs. B," she answers. "You look fantastic."

They laugh together, a purring sound. "Mrs. B," Annika says. "May I use the facilities?"

M kisses my face and my neck. My face fits into his clavicle.

"How did you get here?" I ask him.

"I flew," he answers. "To find you."

M kisses our mother's hands, ridiculously. She holds them to her cheek, lets her mouth go soft. "Oh," she says to him. "You two will have beautiful children."

M looks at me. "Children?" He is unsettled.

I hold up my hands in defense.

"Is there something I should know about?"

Shay and our father walk in. "What should we know?"

M and I huddle together in the hallway. He places his palm flat between my breasts, where the tattoo now is. It is sore, and I make a face. He misunderstands and pulls back his hand. "It seems I haven't seen you in ages," he says. "Funny, huh?"

"Yes," I say. "I know it."

"How are you?" he asks.

"How do I look?"

"Tired," he says. "To tell you the truth."

"I am."

"But good. You look pretty good to me."

"There are things. Things have happened."

"It doesn't matter."

"It does. They do."

"OK, then whatever. Things happen." He touches my face up by the hairline, where it is dry. "I love you."

"Can we go home?"

"Oh, yes," he says. "Whenever. Whenever you want."

★

Our mother pours from a flask into her empty cup, something thick, something purple. Shay looks uncomfortable, and counts to herself. Our mother wipes her mouth, traces the table with her nails and says, "So, M. I've heard so much about you." She sounds sleepy. Her breasts rest on the table.

I try to think of anything I've said. I can remember nothing.

"M," she continues. "So unusual."

"Like James Bond," he says.

Our mother is confused, keeps smiling.

"His boss," he explains. "His boss was named Q."

"I thought there was an M," our father says.

"There was," M says.

"Wasn't the boss named M?"

"No," M says. "Q. M was the one that gave him the gadgets."

"Gadgets?" our mother asks.

"Yeah. Like bombs and guns and cameras that are bombs and guns," he says.

"I'd just like a microwave," our mother says. "That's all."

"P. One was named P," our father says. "And on that note, I'm off to the john."

"Dad," Shay groans.

"Just a microwave. And one of those food choppers," our mother repeats. She looks around, but no one reacts.

M looks exhausted.

Annika takes a polite bite off her plate, then pushes it back towards our mother. "This was delicious, Mrs. B. Thank you so much."

"Oh," our mother says, delighted. "God, you're all grown up. You're so beautiful." Annika blushes somewhat, and our mother looks around, smiling only with her face. Then she looks at the roast. "Thank you, darling," she says to Annika. "But it's just not the same. This is nothing." She pushes the plate back closer to

Annika. "You should have tasted my grandmother's."

"Mrs. Bruscke. It was delicious," M says.

Our mother moves to get the pitcher of water. M bends to my ear. "Where the hell did you come from?" he asks.

I reach over for the plate of food, and begin to eat to fill my mouth. Shay raises an eyebrow at me. Are you OK? she mouths to me.

M whispers again, "Let's go home tonight. Let's elope." He licks at my ear and I push him away, gently. "Come on," he says. "They're awful sweet, but I couldn't take this for twenty-four hours."

Twenty-four hours. "There's something I have to do first," I whisper back.

"Then do it," he says.

"Tina," our father says, sitting back down. "You make a good roast."

"Bill." Our mother waves her hand at him. "You don't remember." She rubs her temples. "The fire."

At that, our family looks at Annika, and it takes a moment for me to realize she's the space Reese would be.

"So many years I tried to reproduce the recipe," our mother continues. "Tried this, tried that. Bought special spices. But grandmother's recipe, poof. Thirty seconds of fire, gone to the ages." Our mother sighs, looks out the window. "And when something is gone, it's gone forever."

Everyone joins her gaze. They watch as if the fire were just now happening outside.

Our mother breaks the silence. "Katey, be a good

girl," she says. "Put up some water for coffee."

I stand up, lay the plate down. Our mother doesn't turn her head, but grabs my arm. "And please," she continues. "You can use the good china."

NINE

Outside the kitchen, the world waits, swollen. I see my reflection in the window panes, the steel kettle. The good coffee set is in a back cabinet, the porcelain yellow with age, velvet with dust.

I run the water and rinse the set. Light glows through each cup, delicate as the conch of an ear.

As the water boils, I scoop instant coffee, two teaspoons each. The silver is discolored with the dye of cough syrups.

Are you OK? Shay mouthed to me. I didn't answer her. Always I said nothing.

My hair falls across my face like insects. I realize I'm shaking. I smooth the strands back. They are thick and they are hollow. "I'm real," I whisper. "I'm real."

I pour from the kettle, the smell of coffee. I only make five cups. The smell of coffee makes me sick.

I watch my reflection again, mouth some more words. What I say is, "I miss her," but it looks like it could be anything, anything at all. Then I look through the window. Only Peter's house, nothing more.

Outside, the world sucks into me. It offers me a homecoming.

The car alarm sets itself off again, working its way into my head like a voice. My mother's voice, Reese's voice, saying, I gave you everything, but now it doesn't matter. I touch my chest; this I take with me, all I have is what I see, what I can remember. I am right here.

I drown out the voices to hear my own. I move to the door for my entrance.

At Don's memorial, we all read the Twenty-third Psalm from xeroxed cards I rolled between my fingers. I bowed my head and pretended that was sadness.

Surely goodness and mercy shall follow me all the days of my life.